THE WILDE BOYS

Right across the West, lawmen were losing their fight against crime. Something had to be done fast. But what?

It was a retired judge named Wilde who came up with the answer – to pit one outlaw against another.

From that point on, his 'law-enforcers' became six of the meanest misfits ever to see the inside of a jail cell; a murderous albino, a black gunfighter, an Apache half-breed, a one-time Pinkerton detective, a Missouri-born conman and a giant whose hands were deadlier than a Gatling gun.

Together they formed a tough-as-knuckles bunch. Those not destined to hang faced life imprisonment. But by becoming the judge's 'Wilde boys', they stood to regain freedom and respect – providing they could survive their first mission, of course; to bring down a kill-crazy tyrant known only in whispers as the Black Wolf ...

The Wilde Boys

BEN BRIDGES

A Black Horse Western

ROBERT HALE · LONDON

© David Whitehead 1988
First published in Great Britain 1988

ISBN 0 7090 3340 0

Robert Hale Limited
Clerkenwell House
Clerkenwell Green
London EC1R 0HT

Photoset in North Wales by
Derek Doyle & Associates, Mold, Clwyd.
Printed in Great Britain by
WBC Print Ltd., Barton Manor, Bristol.
Bound by WBC Bookbinders Limited.

For Mike Linaker,
whose talent as a writer is surpassed
only by his value as a friend.

One

Yuma Penitentiary. Midnight.

Chained to the cold stone floor of his nine foot square cell, Tom Boone came awake to the sound of approaching footsteps and muted voices. He couldn't make out what was being said – he was still half asleep – but when the footsteps stopped outside his cell door he felt a sudden jolt of fear that woke him up fast.

What in hell was going on? Had they decided to bring the date of his execution forward for some reason? Was that what all this was about? Sweet Blessed Mary ...

His ears picked up other sounds then, the rattle of keys on a ring, the sound of one key being slipped into the lock, a click that echoed along the corridor outside.

He tensed.

The cell door swung open and two uniformed guards stepped inside. One of them held a lamp, trimmed low. Its soft yellow glow chased away some of the shadows to reveal cool, mossy walls, a damp, puddled floor with Boone chained at its centre, a scuttling of cockroaches and something larger that might have been rats.

'Wake up, nigger,' said the guard with the lamp.

Boone didn't let them see that he was already awake. In the Yuma Pen, any edge, no matter how small or seemingly insignificant, was an advantage to be grabbed, maybe used later. He huddled on the floor, feigning sleep, until a boot nudged him in the ribs.

'Huh? Wha –'

He did not try to sit up. The chains that shackled his wrists to the floor were not long enough for that. Instead he stared up at the guards who loomed over him, his dark eyes moving from one to the other. The first was a squat, pot-bellied man named Mason. The other was tall, skinny, with a face pocked by some childhood illness. His name was Jellicoe.

It was Jellicoe who spoke. 'All right, Chic,' he said. 'Set him loose.'

Mason found another key on his ring and hunkered down beside Boone with a grunt of effort. As he unlocked the chains he said, 'No false moves now, black boy. Nick here's watchin' you, awright?'

It took Boone a moment to find his voice. 'What's goin' on, Mason?'

Mason froze. 'How's that again, boy?'

Boone bit back a curse, said, 'What's this all about, *Mister* Mason?'

A crooked grin creased Mason's pasty jowls. 'You'll find out.'

'Is it … uh … ?'

'How's that?'

'Uh … They goin' hang me now 'stead of later, Mr Mason? Is that it?'

Mason lifted his heavy shoulders in a shrug. 'Could be.'

Boone let his breath escape in an angry, frustrated sigh. He might've known better than to expect a straight answer from one of the guards. He shut up, lay back on the cold stone floor while Mason took the shackles off him, then slowly sat up as Mason got back on his feet.

'All right, get up,' said Jellicoe.

Boone did as he was told, slowly easing the cramp out of his muscles. When he'd first arrived at the Pen a month before, he'd carried two hundred pounds on his six-four frame. He'd thinned out some in the past couple of weeks, but he still towered over the guards, a big-built man about thirty-five or so, his skin a glistening ebony, his black hair a tight fuzz of curls cropped close to his head, his face passably handsome except for the pale, crooked scar running down his right cheek.

'Outside,' said Jellicoe.

Boone shuffled through the door, the length of his steps dictated by the two-foot chain that joined his ankles. The corridor outside stank of sweat and fear and refuse. Coming at him through the surrounding shadows he heard the coughs and screams and shouts and snores that had plagued him every night, the sounds that always made him think he was sharing a waiting room with passengers bound for hell. Passengers who didn't know they'd already reached their destination.

'What's happenin' out there?' asked one voice.

'Hey, Jelly-belly, that you?' said another. 'Open this goddamn door and maybe we can do us a deal.'

Jellicoe lifted the lamp high with his right hand, balancing a long, wicked-looking baton in his left. 'Get back to sleep, you miserable bastards!' His voice echoed through the night, but did little to quieten the restless prisoners.

Mason prodded Boone in the back to start him moving toward the heavy, barred door at the end of the corridor. Boone obeyed without question.

All right, he thought. So they're going to hang me now 'stead of later. He'd resigned himself to dying a long time ago, but now that the time had finally arrived, he wasn't so sure he could take it. He'd prepared himself for another ten days of life, if existing in this swamp-hole of a prison could be called life. Now he wouldn't even have that long.

He wanted to panic but he knew he mustn't. He had to go out like a man. Lord knew, he hadn't done much in his life that was right. At least he could do this properly.

He passed through the barred doorway and down another stretch of foul-smelling corridor, with the two prison guards clattering along behind him and his shadow skittering around ahead. Jellicoe got them through another heavy, double-locked wooden door and they all stepped out into the moon-washed compound.

Boone shivered.

It was colder still out here, with no protection from the harsh desert chill except his thin grey uniform and a much-repaired set of longjohns, but Boone pulled up sharp, taken aback by the grandeur of the star-picked night spread like black canvas above him.

He shivered again. Then the moment was gone as another push in the back sent him shuffling across the compound toward the administration block fifty yards ahead.

Boone held himself upright, trying his best to salvage whatever remained of his dignity. The night was wide, cold, empty and silent. It held no comfort for him at all.

Around him the prison walls rose up from the desert floor like block after block of moon-washed ice. He'd learned to hate those walls, the four corner guard towers, the deadly, ugly snout of the Gatling gun poking out from the gate tower. God, how he'd learned to hate them.

A tumbleweed wagon, a kind of cell on wheels, stood outside the administration block, with a barred window in each wooden side wall and a heavy, padlocked door at the back. There were two bony-looking horses in the traces, but no-one up on the seat. Other than that, Boone could only see a faint orange glow coming through the curtains of the prison governor's office and a saddled appaloosa tied to the hitch-rack out front.

As they approached the wagon, Mason trotted off ahead, selecting another key with which he opened the back door. Inside there was an ink-splash of shadow, but as Boone climbed the steps and went inside, he could smell sweat and fear and knew he was not alone.

The door closed behind him. The lock clicked shut with a sound like the cocking of a handgun. Then the guards went away.

'Who's that?' asked a voice from the far end of the wagon.

Boone tried to penetrate the darkness with little success. 'Boone.'

'The nigger?'

Boone didn't reply. Instead he asked, 'Anyone else here apart from you, whoever you are?'

They didn't reply straight away. But then, one by one, they gave their names, and he knew from the tone of their voices that no matter how tough they might have been or how determined they were not to let the Pen get to them, they were scared now because they didn't know what to expect next.

'Chance,' said the voice at the end of the carriage. Then, gradually coming closer,

'Forrest.'

'McCord.'

There was a pause. Then the fifth voice said softly, 'Dark.'

Boone didn't acknowledge the introductions, such as they were. He knew them all, even though he hadn't had much to do with any of them. But Dark he knew best of all. One look into that pale, vicious albino's face stayed with a man.

'Know what this is all about, Boone?' McCord asked. He was a tall, slim fellow about thirty-two or three, with a sharp nose, a smiling mouth, bright blue eyes and sandy blond hair. Boone had seen him around a couple of times.

'Was hopin' you could tell me,' he replied.

The conversation died there. A minute passed, stretched into three, five, eight. Then a sound came through the barred windows and the men in the tumbleweed wagon stiffened and peered out through the bars across the compound.

Through the moonlight they could make out three men crossing the hard-packed earth, headed for the wagon. The silhouettes of Mason and Jellicoe were easily recognisable, but the small figure between them remained a mystery. Boone squinted, frowned, said over his shoulder, 'Who's the guy in the centre?'

Dark was the one who spoke. 'The 'breed,' he said shortly.

'Longblade?'

'Uh-huh.'

'I thought he was in the hot-box.'

'Well they let him out, dummy.'

The figures came closer and again Mason trotted ahead to unlock the wagon door. It swung open and the cold, sweaty air inside stirred a little.

Longblade, an Apache half-breed, came to a halt at the foot of the steps, his short, blocky legs planted defiantly.

'Get in there,' Jellicoe growled.

But Longblade didn't move. Everyone in the prison knew he was an ornery cuss. No matter how many times the guards beat him or locked him up in the hot-box, he always came back for more. Maybe he enjoyed it. Or maybe he just wanted to prove that they couldn't break him, no matter what they tried.

'I said get in there,' Jellicoe repeated.

Still the Apache did not move.

Jellicoe hit him in the back with his baton. The length of wood made a solid crack as it struck. Longblade grunted, but that was all. He had nothing against getting into the wagon, he just wanted to be awkward. Jellicoe hit him again and the half-breed started to climb.

But as Longblade filled the doorway, Dark drawled, 'You don't expect us to ride with this chicken-shit half-blood, do you, Mason?'

Dark didn't expect a reply. But he did expect a reaction from the Apache, and he was not disappointed.

The Indian said something in his low guttural tongue, then threw himself at the albino. Within seconds, the wagon's cramped, shadowy interior became an arena for the two men as they tried to kick, punch, gouge and throttle each other to death.

Jellicoe started yelling orders and brandishing his baton, but his voice was lost in the bedlam. Forrest and McCord started yelling encouragement to one or other of the fighters. The wagon began rocking dangerously on old, rusted springs. At last Jellicoe said to Mason, 'All right, get in there and subdue 'em, for crissakes.'

'Who, me?'

'I'll cover you, if that's what you're worried about.'

Seeing that Jellicoe had seniority among the guards, Mason reluctantly clambered into the wagon with his own baton handy and reached out for the Apache. The baton rose and fell. Longblade went limp with a grunt and Dark gave him one more kick in the ribs before Mason was able to cold-cock him with the same deadly efficiency. Then Mason got out of there quickly and Jellicoe shut and bolted the door.

After a while silence settled back over the wagon, although it was not as complete as it had been. Listening to the laboured breathing of the other men, Boone tried to figure out what in hell was going on. Dark, Chance, Forrest, McCord, Longblade and himself. What did they have in common? Why had they all been gathered together like this?

In the prison governor's drab, cluttered office, Deputy United States Marshal Abel Frost drained his third cup of black, bitter coffee and suppressed a shudder.

He was a tall man with a narrow waist and long, slightly bowed legs, and his lean, trail-wise face was dominated by a pair of curious grey eyes and an enormous handlebar moustache. He'd been a lawman for the last seven years and fought Indians with General Crook's Fourteenth Infantry in the eight years before that, was known to be as hard as nails and twice as sharp: but never in his forty-two years had he tasted coffee quite so bad. ∌

Still, in fairness to Governor Tullett, who sat on the other side of the desk, watching him through wide, tired eyes and trying desperately to think up some engaging line of conversation until it was time for Frost to leave, nothing had felt or tasted right to the lawman since he'd been handed his current assignment.

Betrayal did that to a feller.

'Oh dear,' said the governor. He was a small, prissy little man in his mid-fifties who wore his wire-framed spectacles like an out of order sign on his eyes. He was referring to the commotion that had just floated in through the office window. 'I *knew* there'd be trouble,' he muttered, fretting at the celluloid collar of his starched white shirt.

Frost tried to smile reassuringly as he set his empty cup back on its saucer. 'Well, sounds like it's all over now,' he replied.

'Hmmm,' said Governor Tullett non-committally. As he put his elbows on the desk and leaned forward, Frost thought he looked like a baby trying to escape from his play-pen. 'I'm sorry, marshal, but all of this really *is* highly irregular, you know.'

Frost nodded his understanding. But since Tullett had already pointed out the irregularity of what was happening here tonight a dozen times already, the marshal could feel his already-short fuse starting to burn.

'I know,' he replied, trying his damnedest to maintain an air of diplomacy. 'And I understand the fix my orders have put you in, governor. But those orders come from the highest authority –'

Tullett waved a dismissive hand. 'Yes, but –'

'The *highest*,' Frost repeated firmly. He fixed the smaller man with his strange grey eyes and fingered his black-grey moustache for a long pair of seconds until Tullett had quietened down. 'Yeah, this whole business *is* highly irregular,' he went on in understatement. 'But whether you like it or not, governor, the likes of you and me exist only to *follow* orders, not give 'em – leastways not important ones like these.'

'True,' Tullett agreed with a nod. 'Up to a point, that is. But –'

Frost held up his right hand, palm out. Immediately the prison governor fell silent again.

'The thing to remember is this,' Frost said slowly. 'The people who give the orders are the ones who take the blame if things go wrong. There's nothing they can do to the rest of us. We just do what we're told.'

He didn't especially believe that, but it seemed to placate the governor, who was by nature a nervous individual who craved constant reassurance. The smaller man smiled his understanding, then took off his glasses and gave them a wipe with a none-too-clean handkerchief. As he slipped them back on, he indicated the coffee pot on the tray to his left.

'Another cup of coffee, marshal?'

'Uh, not for me, thanks all the same,' Frost replied quickly.

The governor was just about to pour himself a re-fill when there was a knock at the door. Tullett told whoever it was to come in, and Jellicoe entered the room, his cap tucked respectfully under his right arm. The prison guard met Frost's gaze, then let his mud-coloured eyes ooze across to the governor.

'Prisoners're ready to move,' he muttered.

Tullett's relief was obvious. 'Good, good. Uh … we heard some noise a moment ago … ?'

Jellicoe shrugged. 'Couple of the prisoners decided to have a diff'rence of opinion,' he replied. 'I soon sorted it out.'

'Good man, Jellicoe.'

Frost got to his feet and placed his dark blue campaign hat firmly atop his greying thatch. He was somewhere around six-one or two, which meant he was about the same height as Jellicoe but a good ten inches taller than Tullett.

'You all set then, Jellicoe?' Frost asked.

'Sure.'

'Then let's do it.'

Frost turned back to Tullett just as the little man got to his feet, extending his right hand.

'Thanks for your help,' the marshal said, not meaning a word of it.

They shook. 'Anything to help the, ah, highest authority,' Tullett replied with equal lack of conviction.

Frost quit the room and made his way down a

narrow, poorly-lit hallway with Jellicoe following close on his heels. Outside he pulled up sharp to study the moon-washed tumbleweed wagon and shake his head. Beside him, Jellicoe jammed his cap down over his narrow skull.

'Somethin' wrong?' he asked casually.

Frost shrugged. 'No. Nothing.'

Jellicoe studied the lawman's profile. 'Only I get the feelin' you ain't too happy with this deal,' he remarked.

'Oh?'

'Yeah. And I got to admit, it *is* …' He tried to find the right word.

'Highly irregular?' Frost suggested.

'Yeah.'

They stood there a moment longer, then Frost said, 'Come on, Jellicoe. Ours is not to reason why. Besides which, I'm starting to freeze my balls off out here.'

The lawman crossed to the hitch-rack, untied the appaloosa and swung into his McClellan saddle with the ease of a born horseman. As he did so, a voice from outside the wagon said, 'Hey you! What the hell's going on around here?'

Frost walked his horse past the wagon, giving no sign that he had heard the question.

'Hey!' snapped the voice. 'I'm talkin' to you!'

'Well don't,' Frost replied quietly.

Jellicoe hurried to the front of the wagon and hauled himself up onto the seat beside Chic Mason. Mason held the reins and his right foot was resting lightly on the brake, just waiting for the command to move out.

Frost didn't keep him waiting. 'Let's do it,' he said again. They did.

Mason slapped the reins against the animals' rumps. '*Giddap there!*'

The wagon pulled away from the admin block with a jerk that threw the six prisoners all over the inside of the portable cell. Hearing them cuss, Jellicoe and Mason allowed themselves a quiet chuckle. Frost, riding slightly ahead and to the left, did not join in. His mind was elsewhere.

At the main gate, beneath the impassive stare of the Gatling gun's ten barrels, another guard checked Frost's authorisation. Frost stifled a yawn as the guard skimmed through his orders, reading by lamp-light. Then the command was given for the gates to be opened, and someone inside the wagon said, 'Hey, you guys – we're gettin' *out* of here!'

Someone else loosed off a rebel yell.

'Keep it down!' roared Jellicoe, hammering on the roof of the cell with his baton.

Slowly, the heavy gates swung open to reveal a flat, sage-studded desert floor shimmering in the moonlight beyond the prison. Frost gave a small sigh and tipped his hat to the guard at the gate, then kicked his appaloosa into motion. The tumbleweed wagon rattled along behind him like a faithful old hound.

The prison had been built on the east bank of the Colorado River, where it joined the Gila. It was the Gila they followed as it wound a chuckling course eastward, heading roughly in the direction of Phoenix, about a hundred and fifty miles away.

Around them, the land spread out like a wrinkled blanket, dotted here and there with bunch grass, prickly pear and giant cacti. The night crouched overhead, clear, fine and ice-cold. The marshal used his left hand to button his jacket against the raw air, his teeth tightly clenched.

Betrayal, he thought again. He was thinking about his so-called friends and colleagues in the US marshal's office in Tucson.

They've eased me right out, he told himself. They think I'm too old so they've brushed me aside with a crazy mission that can only end in disaster. And no matter what I just told Tullett, when that disaster finally happens, I'll get the blame, not the bastard who gave the original orders!

And that's just what they want – an excuse to fire me. *Damn*!

For an hour, maybe two, the wagon rumbled across the vast, sleeping desert. Few words were spoken. There wasn't really much worth saying. The six prisoners swayed back and forth in silence, each of them pondering his fate and wondering if he would live to see another daybreak.

A minute dragged into two, three, ten.

And then each of the prisoners stiffened as they felt the wagon begin to slow and finally stop. In the airless silence Boone heard the tense, expectant breathing of the other men and knew he was every bit as keyed up himself.

'What's goin' on?' Dark called up to the guards. There was no reply.

Boone and McCord strained their vision at one of the barred windows, while Chance and Dark tried their luck at the other. Only Forrest and Longblade appeared not to give a damn about the whole crazy business. But then even Forrest was moved to ask, albeit without much enthusiasm, 'See anything?'

'Nah,' McCord replied. 'Leastways nothing much. A building, maybe.'

'Another jail?'

'Maybe. Looks … kinda looks like a fort. Couple of buildings, walls, a gate.'

'Walls?'

'Yeah, you know. Walls. Buildings have 'em to stop the roof from caving in.'

Forrest made a sound of impatience. 'Ah, get outta the way and let me take a look for myself.'

At the other window, Dark narrowed his ratty pink eyes as he caught sight of Frost walking his appaloosa slowly toward the gateway of what indeed appeared to be some sort of garrison.

'Who's the dude on the horse?'

'How the hell do I know?' Chance replied testily.

'Keep it down in there!' Jellicoe roared from above.

'Blow it out your nose!' Dark yelled back.

A few muttered words floated back to them on the crisp night air, coming from the gateway, but nothing they could understand. Then the six men heard the squeak of a rusty hinge and they knew that someone inside the fort was hauling the gate open. Without warning the wagon jerked into motion again, scattering the cursing inmates.

The wagon passed through the gate.

'Outta one jail and into another,' Dark muttered in disgust.

Boone peered up at the roof of the wagon, as if he could actually see beyond the thick, iron-strapped planks at what lay outside. 'I ain't so sure,' he said quietly.

'Huh?'

The negro shrugged. 'I don't know. Just a feelin'.'

Behind them, the heavy gate slammed with a roar like thunder.

Two

A minute or so later, Mason set his weight down on the brake and the wagon came to a halt. The prisoners heard and felt the guards climbing down from the high seat, but no-one spoke. One thing was sure, though – they'd arrived at wherever it was they'd been headed.

In a second McCord was back at the nearest window, his handsome features silvered by what little moonlight filtered into the cell.

'See anything now?' Forrest asked in his usual gruff manner.

'Nah,' McCord replied sourly. 'Apart from starlight, the whole place is in darkness.'

'Huh?'

As Forrest sat up, they all heard the metallic scrape of a key in a padlock and their attention turned to the bolted door. A second later it swung open with a dry creak of protest to reveal Jellicoe and Mason standing at the foot of the steps, Mason hefting a wicked-looking Greener shotgun.

'Out,' barked Jellicoe.

With a deliberation purposely designed to

irritate the guards, the six prisoners slowly got to
their feet and climbed out of the wagon amidst a
rattle of ankle-chains. Once out in the open, they
stood hugging themselves against the chill that
seeped through their thin prison-issue denims,
looking around at the dark, silent garrison in
which they now found themselves.

'What *is* this place?' McCord asked, his voice
unusually subdued. 'A fort?'

The answer was so obvious that Jellicoe didn't
bother to reply. Of course it was a fort. Well, an
outpost, at least. It measured about a hundred
and twenty feet square and its walls stood fifteen
feet high. The parade ground was edged with neat
rows of round, fist-sized rocks. At its centre stood
a tall, now-empty flagpole.

The men squinted through the darkness.

The wagon had pulled up outside a long, low
building with a porch overhang, presumably a
barracks of some kind. Directly opposite and to
their right stood more buildings, a stable and
another, smaller gate that led into an adobe-
walled corral.

Everywhere they looked, everything they saw,
was cloaked in shadow and grave-quiet. There
wasn't even any sign of the guy who'd opened up
the gates for them, or the big dude on the
appaloosa, although the horse itself was tied to
the hitch-rack in front of the barracks.

With his baton, Jellicoe indicated that very
building. His harsh, slightly nasal voice cut
through the air. 'All right – inside.'

Mason back-pedalled, bringing up the double-barrelled shotgun. The six convicts shuffled into the building.

The room they stepped into was about twenty-five feet by fifteen, and through the gloom they could just about discern the shapes of six bunks, three to either wall with enough space between to accommodate low, square wooden lockers.

McCord whistled. Chance asked what in hell was going on. The rest just looked around in awe, unaccustomed to such luxury after the harsh living conditions of Yuma Pen. Forrest, content just to take whatever came his way, flopped onto the last bunk on the left. McCord immediately claimed the next one along. Dark turned to face the two guards, who stood just outside the doorway. Had they been able to see it, his bleached, hawkish face showed anger, distrust and not a little fear.

'Just what in hell *is* goin' on here?' he snapped.

Before Jellicoe or Mason could reply, a match flared just inside and to the left of the doorway, and Dark jumped. In the sudden blossom of flame, the six prisoners saw the tall, thin man who had accompanied them from the Pen on horseback.

Without a word he reached up to a lantern hanging from one low rafter and as he got it working, an amber glow spilled sluggishly into the room, dissolving most of the existing shadows and creating six new ones.

Six pairs of eyes looked into one unsettling grey pair.

Then Dark spoke. 'Who the hell're you? An'
where the hell are we?'

Raking his eyes across the six men, Abel Frost
felt more certain than ever that his latest
assignment was doomed to failure. He looked
from Forrest, sprawled on his bunk without a care
in the world, into McCord's idiot grin; from the
glittering challenge in Dick Chance's eyes to the
open disdain on Longblade's flat, coppery face;
from the curiosity of the big negro, Boone, to his
exact opposite, Nathan Dark, the albino.

He sighed. Killers and thieves the lot of them,
he thought, exactly the kind of trail-scum he'd
spent seven long years tracking down and sending
to prison. And worse, at least from his point of
view, they were all lone wolves, so Lord knew how
he was supposed to mould them into the special
fighting force Washington had ordered him to
create.

Looking at them now, looking into their flat,
calculating eyes, Frost decided he wouldn't put it
past any of them to back or gut-shoot him just for
the hell of it. But that was okay, because when he
had to, he could play the same rotten game as
hard and as dirty as the worst of them.

'My name is Frost,' he said at last. 'I'm a United
States Marshal. And from now on, you call this
place home.'

Six faces showed frowns of puzzlement.

'Huh?'

'What?'

'Yeah, what's goin' on, marshal?'

Frost held up his right hand. '*Shut it!*' he growled.

Much to his surprise, they did.

'All right, so you're curious,' he said, treating each of them in turn to his penetrating gaze. 'Be patient. You'll get all the answers you want, in the morning.' He ignored the sudden rumble of dissent. 'For now, all you need to know is this. The only ones among you not sentenced to hang in the next two weeks face life imprisonment. Hard labour. To be honest with you, I don't know which is worse. But as of now, you've got a reprieve. It's up to you to decide whether or not it's only temporary. From now on, you answer to me. I'm the boss. Do what I tell you and we'll get along fine. But if any one of you steps out of line, you *all* go back to the Pen. Got it?'

Chance licked his lips. Boone instinctively felt at his throat. Only Dark seemed unimpressed. He pointed to the two-foot chain that joined his ankles. 'How 'bout takin' these off, marshal?'

Frost glanced down. 'As soon as I think you've earned it, they'll be removed,' he replied. 'Until then, they can stay where they are.'

Dark scowled. He was about five feet ten and a hundred and forty pounds. In his prison uniform he looked like a scarecrow, an impression reinforced by his bloodless skin, snow-white hair and rodent-pink eyes.

'Hey, know what I think, marshal?' he asked

mockingly. 'I think you'd be a sight less
high-and-mighty if Jellicoe and Mason weren't
here to back you up.'

As Frost allowed a sepulchral smile to play
across his lips, he fingered his handlebar
moustache, a sure sign to those who knew him
that trouble was coming.

'You do, huh?' he asked.

Dark's face split in a cocksure grin. 'Yeah, I do.'

Frost looked into the albino's ugly face. He felt
scratchy enough as it was. He didn't need a
smart-ass to make his life any worse. Down at his
side, his left fist began to clench. But then,
suddenly, he relaxed. As much as he wanted to see
how many of Dark's teeth he could shake loose, he
did not want to fall into the trap of becoming
manipulated by the white-faced trouble-maker.

He moved slowly towards the doorway. 'I guess
it's about three am right now,' he said, addressing
them all. 'I'd bed down if I were you guys. Up
again at dawn.'

Dark came forward. 'Hey, Frost. Didn't you
hear what I said?'

'Sure,' Frost replied. 'I ain't deaf.' He glanced
over the albino's shoulder at the other men.
'Remember what I said. Stand by me and you'll be
all right. Foul up and you go back to the Pen, and
whatever fate awaits you.'

Before any of them could speak again, Frost
turned and left the room. The half-dozen from hell
listened to him go, still standing or lounging
exactly as they had during the entire exchange.

Then the guards withdrew, slamming, locking, then bolting the door behind them. A moment later, shutters were closed over the room's two windows and padlocked tight.

'Well,' Chance muttered to Dark, 'you sure made a big impression there.'

'Ah, shuddup,' Dark replied. 'At least I tried to get some answers outta him. Where were the rest of you?'

No-one replied.

'What do you figure it's all about?' Chance asked, directing his question to the albino, who seemed to have become their leader.

Dark ran a hand through his shock-white hair. 'I don't know. Somethin' federal, since a US Marshal's involved.'

'But *what*?' Boone asked.

'How the hell do I know?' Dark snapped. He liked the idea of playing boss. He didn't like being asked questions he couldn't answer so much. 'Look, you heard what the guy said. We'll find out in the mornin', okay? Just quit jawin' and let's get some sleep.'

One by one the men looked around the room, at the plain green walls and the freshly-swept plank floor, then settled on their chosen bunks to stare up at the still-shadowed rafters. All, that was, except for Dark.

'What's up now?' McCord asked irritably.

The albino glared down at him in the uncertain light of the single lantern. '*You*,' he replied, waving one hand at the empty cot next to McCord.

'I hear tell you're a faggot, McCord. If they think I'm sleepin' anywhere near you, they got another think comin'.'

As silence thickened the air, blood boiled up into McCord's face. 'The hell you say!' he roared, swinging up off his bunk. The others watched him closely, for they had heard the same rumours. 'Maybe we ought to get a couple things straight around here. After all, I ain't that keen on sharing with a goddamn freak.'

In less than a second McCord and Dark came together in a flurry of punches, and the other men, half-relieved by the way things were shaping up and excited by the prospect of some action, started cheering them on again, exactly the way they had when Dark had locked horns with Longblade inside the tumbleweed wagon.

The two combatants now fell away from each other, fists up, ankle-chains rattling, searching for new openings. Both men, having pretty much the same height, weight and reach, were fairly evenly matched, but Dark was older by about six years and had had more experience at bare-knuckle brawling.

So it was he who came in as fast as his chains would allow, hammering away for all he was worth. One hard, pale fist caught McCord a stinging blow on the nose, and he took a step back, blinking tears out of his faded blue eyes and wiping blood from his nostrils and upper lip.

'*Attaboy, Dark! Give 'im hell!*'

'*Keep your guard up, McCord!*'

'Finish 'im, for chrissakes!'

The antagonists locked bright, angry eyes across the four feet that separated them, both breathing hard. Then McCord came in again and this time he kept his head tucked down into his shoulders and his fists up and moving. He barrelled into Dark and hit him with a left-right-left-right combination to the ribs.

Dark grunted a little and began to fold. But when he was eye-level with the blond's groin, he suddenly bunched his right fist and let him have it straight in the crotch.

To give him credit, McCord fought down the yelp of pain before it could explode from his throat. But there was no way he could stop himself from doubling over in agony.

Dark, straightening up again and sensing victory, slammed his right knee into the other man's face, and McCord fell backward, stumbled, was kept off-balance by a right jab in the stomach and a left hook to the jaw.

While McCord continued to stumble around on legs like jelly, Dark quickly palmed sweat off his face. The cheering and whistling around him had died down a little, but he no longer needed it to spur him on. As he came in for the kill, he looked more like a rat than ever, with his nostrils flared and his eyes blood-red.

McCord bent before him, clutching at his groin, beaten and defenceless.

But before the albino could reach his target, Forrest stepped between them. Forrest was in his late thirties, six feet two, two-twenty pounds, with a tanned, battered face beneath a shaggy black beard and slitted, coffee-brown eyes. He was known around the Pen as an easy-going guy, but when crossed he always made it a point to exact swift and sometimes terrible retribution.

Silence poured over the scene. Then Forrest said quietly, 'Back off.'

Under any other circumstances, Dark would have done just that. He was as ornery as the best of them, but he wasn't so stupid as to take on a man eighty pounds heavier than he was, at least not hand-to-hand and without a set of knuckle-dusters to give him an edge.

But these were not other circumstances. He'd just become leader of this pack. He wasn't going to be dethroned just on Forrest's account, no matter how much muscle he had backing him up.

He was quite literally fighting mad. He stared into Forrest's nearly-hidden eyes just as the larger man reached up to scratch his beard with the short, thick fingers of his liver-spotted left hand.

'Or what?' Dark sneered.

Forrest moved so quickly that none of the men, least of all Dark, was ready for what happened next. The big man bent double, grabbed Dark's ankle-chain in his right hand and pulled. The albino's legs came out from under him and he landed with a crash, hard on his butt.

Boone was the first to start laughing, then Chance and finally McCord. Even Longblade cracked a smile. Dark just glared up at Forrest and spat.

'*Bastard!*'

Nobody heard the clatter of approaching footsteps, or the barrack-room door being unlocked. The first they knew that all the noise had drawn unwanted attention was when Frost, Jellicoe and Mason poured into the room. This time Mason was not the only one holding a shotgun.

The laughter stopped. The room fell silent.

Frost looked at each of the prisoners in turn. Since he didn't need a fancy college education to work out what had been going on, he didn't bother to ask. But the sight of Nathan Dark flat on his ass dissipated a little of his anger. That little bastard had had it coming a long time.

The tight-lipped albino climbed slowly to his feet beneath Frost's cold stare, wiping his palms on his pants. Without taking his eyes off the convict, the marshal said over his shoulder, 'Jellicoe. It seems like a little freedom has gone to these fellers' heads.'

Jellicoe nodded. 'Yeah. Seems like.'

The six prisoners concentrated their hard-eyed gaze on the lawman, waiting grimly for whatever came next. Sure enough, Frost began to finger his bushy moustache ominously. Trouble was brewing.

'Get on over to my quarters,' the lawman said, still addressing Jellicoe. 'Just behind the door you'll find six pairs of handcuffs in my warbag.'

The prisoners began to frown. Frost's voice cut through the sudden buzz of half-baked threats.

'From now on I want every man here cuffed to his bunk before lights-out. Got that?'

'Sure.'

'Then do it,' Frost snapped. As Jellicoe left the room, Frost glared at the six sour faces lined up before him, then turned away. On his way out, he paused in the doorway and his mouth turned up in a smile as cold as his name. 'Sleep well, boys,' he said pleasantly. 'See you at sun-up.'

It seemed that no sooner was each man cuffed to his bunk and locked into the now-dark barrack-room than the first grey promise of dawn came filtering through the shuttered windows. Certainly, when Jellicoe and Mason next appeared, bursting in to wake them by the subtle means of hammering at two black and dented pots with their batons, the prisoners awoke tired, cramped and scratchy.

With Jellicoe by the door, covering his partner with a shotgun, Mason moved from bed to bed, uncuffing each prisoner in turn. Only when he had retired a safe distance were they allowed to stand and stretch, then reluctantly remake their hard, narrow cots. They washed in the icy water of the bath-house next door to their sleeping quarters, and were then marched in single file across the silent parade ground.

With the land now bathed in the pale, golden light of a new-born day, they were able to see the outpost in more detail. Their barracks was set into the north-facing wall, opposite a messhall, ordnance shop and the stable. To their left lay other buildings: a guardhouse, blacksmith's shop and, in a regular Army outfit, what would have been officers' quarters. But the six convicts, their guards and Abel Frost, wherever the hell *he* was, appeared to be the garrison's sole inhabitants.

'Hey, Jellicoe, where *is* everybody?'

'Yeah. We here alone, Mister Mason?'

'Shut up!'

Once inside the small empty messhall, Mason dished up bacon, beans and biscuits, better by far than the slops the men had grown used to inside the Pen, but still they found reasons to bitch. It seemed like the thing to do.

As Forrest stoically set about demolishing his first meal of the day, McCord, who was seated next to him at the creaky trestle table, leaned across and said in a whisper, 'Hey, listen. I didn't get a chance to say thanks for helping me out.'

Forrest frowned. 'Huh?'

'You know. Last night.'

'Oh, yeah.' The big man shrugged and spooned up another mouthful of beans.

'Not that I couldn't have handled that bloodless freak,' McCord went on, indicating Dark with a jerk of his chin. 'He just caught me with a lucky punch, otherwise I'd've slaughtered him. But I guess he would have done me some real damage if you hadn't ...'

'Yeah, yeah, all right. I get the picture.'

'Well, I'm just saying,' McCord replied. 'I mean,

I wouldn't want you getting the wrong idea about me, friend. Sure, I've heard those rumours about me. But they're bullshit. I got girls in eight states to vouch for that.'

'Good for you.'

'Well, just so you know,' McCord smiled. He chewed on a spoonful of beans, then bit into a biscuit that tasted more like a cork. 'Hey, you know something? I got the feeling me and you are gonna be good buddies, big feller.'

'Sure.'

'No, I mean it. We get along, see eye to eye. We ...'

'Pilgrim,' Forrest cut in, pushing his empty plate away and reaching for the cup of stewed coffee Mason had given to each man. 'Do me a favour, will you?'

McCord's smile broadened. 'Sure. Name it.'

'Go take a walk.'

A short while later, once the men had been forced at shotgun-point to clean up after them, they were lined up outside in single file with Mason in front and Jellicoe at the rear, then marched past the ordnance shop and stable towards a long, low admin block directly opposite the two closed outpost gates. The sun was climbing steadily now; already the prison denims clung to their backs and turned dark at armpits and chest.

It was as they crossed the parade ground, headed for the admin block, that Chance saw the woman.

'Hey, you guys! Take a look at that!'

Following Chance's pointing finger, the other men saw the woman watching them through one of the dusty windows of the officers' quarters. She looked pretty but pale, in her mid to late-twenties, with curly auburn hair cut to shoulder length and wide, dark eyes, but beyond that her features were lost in the gloom.

Still, a woman was a woman. And to men who had been a long time from the well …

No sooner had he seen her than Dark's face was distorted by a leer. 'Hey, little missy, why'n't you come out an' play a while?'

That was a cue for he, Chance and McCord to batter the woman with such a riot of laughter, cat-calls and whistlings that she hurriedly withdrew from sight.

'That's enough!' yelled Mason.

But Dark was not going to be out-done. He stepped out of line and started toward the officers' quarters, his ankle-chains scraping together in the dust. 'Hey, come on back, honey!'

'Get back in line!' roared Jellicoe.

Dark ignored him, already halfway across to the window at which the girl had been standing.

'*Dark*!' Jellicoe yelled. 'Get back here right now!'

The albino glanced over his shoulder, treating the guard to a wolfish smile. 'Why? What you gonna do, Jelly – shoot me?'

As if in reply, a gunshot cracked the early-morning stillness at exactly that moment, exploding a spray of sand between the albino's feet and causing him to take a sudden, drunken step back and spin around.

'What in –?'

Abel Frost had appeared in the admin block doorway, a New Line Police .38 still smoking in his right hand. He stood tall in the shadow of the porch overhang, and the men could see the anger flaring in his eyes even from this distance.

'Get back in line,' he said quietly.

Dark was frozen to the spot, the gunblast still ringing in his ears. His red eyes, which had been heavy-lidded with lust a moment before, were now every bit as furious as those of the lawman.

'Sonofabitch,' he muttered.

'Do it,' Frost said calmly.

He cocked the single-action Colt, ready for another shot.

The prisoners stood in silence, looking from one man to the other. The hatred between them was so strong that Boone thought he might be able to reach out and touch it.

Dark glared at the marshal.

Frost brought his gun up,

'Awright, awright, fer crissakes,' the albino snapped. 'I'm goin'. Just keep that thing polite!'

He sauntered back to the other men with a wide grin nailed to his face, his attitude conveying nothing of the tension that still jarred the beat of his heart. Frost's eyes burned into him; not until he had taken up his place in the line did the marshal slip his gun back into leather. Then he turned around and disappeared inside the admin block without another word.

'Sonofabitch,' Dark muttered again.

'All right,' barked Jellicoe. '*Move!*'

They did, reluctantly, their feet kicking up little puffs of dust.

Some of the nighttime cold still clung to the ante-room into which they were marched and told to sit. Frost was waiting for them on a raised platform before a large blackboard. Dark gave him a drop-dead look as he came through the door and slumped into the nearest of six folding chairs. Frost only smiled.

The room was about twelve feet square and a dull chocolate brown, but clean enough and full of echoes. A second door to the left of the blackboard led into another, unmarked room that might well have been a CO's office, but no charts, maps or rosters adorned the walls as they would have had the garrison been in any kind of regular use.

Looking around, Boone decided that the room reminded him of the schoolhouse his two children had attended in another, happier time that had no place in the Godawful here-and-now. But memories of his son and daughter always cut him deep, so he shoved them from his mind as he had learned to do ever since his whole life had fallen apart two long years before.

Mason, the last man in, closed the outer door behind him, planted his blocky legs firmly and stood with the shot-gun cradled across his ample belly.

'Hey, marshal,' Dark said, grinning. 'Who was

the she-male?'

'Yeah, she your old lady, marshal?'

Frost's narrow smile was not a thing of beauty. 'All right, you sorry-looking bastards, vacation's over. This is where you start earning your freedom.'

'You call this freedom?' Chance replied.

'You gonna make a speech up there, marshal?' Dark asked sarcastically. 'Christ, I do hate speechifying!'

'No speeches,' Frost replied evenly. 'Just a few words about why you're here.'

That got their attention, all right. Suddenly they were sitting forward, alert, wary, curious.

'Let's start off by getting one thing straight,' Frost said. 'I don't expect any of us to get along like blood brothers, and if I was a religious man I'd thank God, because friends like you cold-blooded sonsofbitches I can *certainly* do without. But for what's been decided for you,' he went on, 'we don't especially need to like each other. It's enough that we do the job.'

That was a lie, of course. A little co-operation would help Frost out no end, but if they knew that, these men would make certain it never happened just to spite him.

'What job?' Chance asked.

It got so quiet in the room that they all heard the buzzing of a single fly up around the smoke-stained ceiling.

The men sat watching Frost expectantly.

He said, 'You're a bunch of thieves, killers, con

men and troublemakers, right?'

No-one replied. There was no need.

'So?' said Dark.

A cemetery smile crossed Frost's dark, lived-in face. 'So you're being given another chance to do what you do best,' he replied quietly.

Three

At exactly that moment, in a little Mexican village about ninety miles southwest, two men were about to die.

Not that they had ever considered the possibility of their own deaths, of course, for their business had always been the deaths of others.

They were bounty hunters.

They entered Tacalima from the north, just as the sun began to rise in the east. Unaware of death's stealthy approach, the townsfolk, of which there were no more than fifty or so, continued to sleep or stir quietly beneath their blankets.

As villages went, Tacalima was not much to look at; a jumble of crude, whitewashed adobe shacks, a few stores, a cantina. There was nothing that would ever make it special, except maybe the eerie, disused monastery that sat fortress-like atop a sage-choked rise about a mile to the west, and so it just sat smack in the middle of the Sonoran Desert, resigned to a slow, lingering demise.

The two bounty hunters reined in before a small

livery stable, empty this early save for a dubious
selection of ribby horses and a couple of mules.
Both men were in their mid-thirties and sweating
heavily even at this comparatively cool hour. They
were very much two of a kind; hard and capable
and not at all nice to know.

The smaller of the two was Ben Cole. He was
clean-shaven, slightly overweight and carried a
Remington Army .44. His partner, Jess Vincent,
was pale despite a life conducted largely out of
doors, and his moustache and sideburns were
blond and fine. He favoured a pair of Dance
Brothers revolvers.

While Vincent led his horse into the livery,
Cole, still mounted, scanned the dusty street. The
only sign of life was a bony dog stretched out in
the shade of a nearby Joshua tree.

Vincent came back out into the strengthening
sunlight. His expression was difficult to read, but
to Cole it looked a lot like doubt.

'What's up now?' Cole asked.

Unable to put it into words, Vincent shrugged.

'Look, I told you,' Cole hissed. 'We know where
to find 'em. We know what to do. What's the
problem?'

Jess Vincent studied his partner carefully,
squinting up at him from out of his thin, pale face.
He and Cole went back a long way, but this was
the first time Jess had shown anything less than
complete faith in his partner's judgement.

'You sure this information's good, Ben?' he
asked.

'Of course it's good!' Cole replied impatiently. 'You heard what the guy had to say for himself, didn't you? Ol' Pancho, he's run a no-account little cantina out here in the middle o' no-place for damn near twelve years. Poor bastard's been a loser all his life. But now he's got the chance to change all that. All of a sudden he's got two owlhoots worth more than three thousand dollars spendin' damn near every Saturday night who-opin' it up and then sleepin' it off at his place!'

'Yeah, but can he be trusted?' Vincent wanted to know.

'Sure he can be trusted!'

Anxious to get on with it, Cole walked his horse a pace along the street before noticing that Vincent was still firmly planted where he'd left him.

'What now?' Cole demanded.

Another shrug. 'I dunno, Ben … Lobo and Jarvis … I mean, they're big league.'

'Sure they're big league. That's why they're worth three grand.'

'But supposing their men …'

'Their men do their drinkin' up at the monast'ry. By the time they come a-runnin', we'll be long gone.'

'And Pancho?'

'Pancho'll tell 'em he didn't see a thing. He was asleep out back when Lobo and his sidekick took off.'

'You think Lobo's men'll fall for that?'

Ben Cole swallowed the insult before it could

spill out and cause a rift that neither man would welcome. But he started to wonder about Vincent's grit. After all, Jess had seemed fine until now. Now he was starting to display a reluctance that Cole had never seen before.

Still, maybe that was because this deal promised to be different from all the rest. For a start, Pancho had come to *them*, had somehow tracked them down in Sonoita in order to put his proposition to them.

And what a proposition, Cole remembered. Jess had shown no reluctance at going up against the infamous 'El Lobo Negro' then. The only thing Jess had shown interest in was the reward money the two outlaws would fetch, a considerable sum, even allowing for a three-way split.

Ben Cole frowned. Jess wasn't usually given to presentiments. Why should he balk now? The plan was as sweet as sugar; take the outlaws by surprise and force them at gunpoint to saddle up and ride for the border, with their gang, stationed up in the monastery, none the wiser.

Money in the bank.

But before Cole could say more, Vincent said, 'Okay. I go round back, get the drop on 'em.'

'Right. But don't do anything 'til I give the word.'

Vincent looked bleak. 'Got it.'

He disappeared down the alley between the stable and the row of stores, leaving Cole to count off a slow sixty seconds before he began to walk his horse along Tacalima's single street towards Pancho's miserable-looking cantina.

As he dismounted, he glanced casually from one shack to the next. If any of the locals were watching him, they were doing a damn good job of it.

Tying his horse to the hitch-rack outside, he entered the cool, dark cantina without hesitation and strode up to the scarred plank-and-barrel counter. Pancho, a small, balding *peon* with a dark complexion and a shadow of stubble, was standing behind the bar, sweating like a pig in his plain cotton shirt and baggy, off-white pants.

Ben Cole met his gaze and held it for a heartbeat before Pancho's black eyes flickered to the left, toward an archway behind the bar that was hung with a curtain of coloured beads. Cole nodded faintly; Jess was out back, waiting.

Cole ordered coffee and slapped coins down on the bar-top. Pancho poured from a pot on the stove. Cole drank the coffee in three gulps and asked for another. This he took to a corner table, where he sat toying with the mug. Only once did he look at the cantina's other two patrons, and even then it was little more than a glance.

But in his guts he felt a tingle of excitement, for Pancho had told it straight that night in Sonoita. Sitting across from him now was undoubtedly Joshua Thorne, the notorious 'Black Wolf' himself, and his smaller, slighter kill-crazy partner in crime, Texas Bob Jarvis.

Ben Cole felt his lips dry up. Those two bastards controlled the meanest bunch of cut-throats since Quantrill went out a-hunting. But now here they were, right in front of him, still bleary-eyed from their Saturday night drunk, just waiting for him to turn them into three grand's worth of dead meat.

But almost immediately he cautioned himself. No. No killing. At least not this close to the monastery on the hill. The last thing Cole wanted was to bring Lobo's ten or fifteen killers down on him. No, nice and quiet, at gunpoint, just like they'd agreed.

Ben scratched his right hand, then reached out to lift the steaming mug to his lips. Catching the eyes of the men he was about to ambush, he nodded a greeting. And suppressed a shudder.

Joshua Thorne, *El Lobo Negro*, was a massive, slab-shouldered negro who could have been any age between thirty and fifty. His skin was a deep, flat black-brown that seemed to eat up light, for it gave back no faint reflection or sheen of sweat. His eyes were brown too, with the whites shot through with scores of tiny broken blood vessels. His hair was tight and black, his sideburns long and speckled with grey. He was dressed in a faded calico shirt and denims, with a bandolier stuffed with shells hanging across the back of his chair. He wore a gunbelt, but Cole could not see the make or condition of the weapon he kept there. He did see the lethal-looking Bowie blade in its sheath on his right hip, however.

His partner was a white man about thirty-one or two, who stood five and a half feet in height and carried scarcely ninety pounds on his spare frame.

Folks called him Texas Bob because he shot them if they accidentally referred to him as Crazy Bob, a nickname by which he was far better known. He dressed soberly in a dusty black suit and cloud-white shirt, and a face that was thin and yellow and eyes that looked bleached of life gave him a weird, spectral appearance. He made no effort to return Ben Cole's greeting, although Thorne gave a smile that revealed chipped, fang-like teeth.

Wolf's teeth. *Lobo*.

Cole's smile died a little then, because he knew the reputations of both these men. He knew there was no crime, no offence too low for them to consider or attempt.

He got up and strode back to the bar, where Pancho, who had wanted the reward money but could not find the guts to kill for it, looked fit to drown in his own sweat.

'Hey, you. Got any rooms for rent around here?'

Pancho cleared his throat. 'Uh ... no, *senor*.'

'Nowhere?'

'No, *senor*.'

'Damn,' Cole muttered in disgust.

It was all an act, of course, cultivated to throw his potential victims off their guard. To them he would appear no more than a drifter who hadn't given them a second thought.

'Well ... How far to Caborca?'

'A ... about a hundred kilometres, *senor*.'

Cole nodded. 'Okay. Give me a bottle of whiskey, will you?'

Pancho did and Cole paid for it.

'*Gracias, amigo.*'

He picked up the bottle in his right hand, another trick he had learned to make his targets lower their guard, and with another nod to the two outlaws, crossed the room and stepped out into the now-harsh sunlight.

The whiskey bottle was hitting the warm sand as he burst back in. His right hand was now filled with iron.

'All right, you bastards! *Hold it*!'

At the same moment, Jess Vincent came through the rattling curtain of beads.

Pancho froze. This was the moment he had been dreading. But he did not quite get to see what happened next.

Crazy Bob Jarvis came up out of his chair and in his left hand he held a Remington New Model Army .44. Since he had been facing the bar, he went straight for Jess. Gunblasts filled the air. Grey smoke lifted to the low ceiling. Chips of plaster flew off the wall beside the outlaw as he triggered his first shot.

The bullet punched a hole into Jess's left shoulder. He staggered and gave a yell, but he knew he wasn't going to die from the wound so he brought his right-side .44 up on Jarvis's chest.

But he didn't fire it.

He didn't get the chance.

Jarvis had already changed his aim. Now his Remington's eight-inch barrel was pointed at Jess's forehead.

He fired.

Jess went backward in a spray of crimson and when he hit the floor, his boots kicked one last tattoo before he died.

The Black Wolf paid no attention to Vincent's final seconds. The minute Ben Cole had walked out the door, he had eased his .31 calibre Colt Wells Fargo from its holster and when Ben burst back in, triggered three slugs in rapid succession.

They all hit Ben in the chest.

The bounty hunter jerked under the impacting lead, fired twice, dug splinters out of the floor with both slugs. As he slid down the wall, already dead, he left three trails of blood to mark his passage.

Silence.

When their ears stopped ringing, the survivors heard the bony dog yapping outside. Pancho stared bug-eyed at the two bodies littering his floor. Thorne and Jarvis busied themselves reloading. Jarvis finished first and peered cautiously out into the street. One or two of the locals had stepped out into the sunlight to see what was going on.

'Any more of 'em?' Thorne asked. He had a voice like overhead thunder.

'Nah.' Jarvis sounded disappointed.

He slipped his Remington back into its holster. 'Hey, Pancho. More whiskey.'

The bartender made no move. He was looking at the bodies and thinking about reward money. Reward money he would not now be able to collect. He wanted to cry.

'*Pancho!*'

'Ah, *si, senores!*'

'More whiskey.'

'And clear this mess up,' Thorne growled.

Pancho hurriedly, and regrettably, did as he was told.

A hush fell over the ante-room as the men digested what Frost had just told them. Then: 'What do you mean, we're bein' given another chance to do what we do best?' asked Nathan Dark, the albino.

Frost told them exactly what he meant, and in actually giving voice to his latest assignment, he could see just how ill-fated it really was. But as dispirited as he felt, he did not allow his personal feelings to enter into it. He had always believed in his job, taken it seriously and carried out orders even when he considered them half-assed. For better or worse, that was the kind of man he was.

So he told the six prisoners that because conventional law-enforcement agencies were proving unable to deal effectively with the growing criminal element, Washington, or, more accurately a recently-retired judge named Isaac Wilde, had decided to try a new approach; to fight fire with fire.

'You mean use outlaws – to fight outlaws?' McCord asked.

When Frost nodded, Chance said, 'You gotta be kiddin', marshal. That's just about the craziest idea I ever heard.'

Frost had to agree, if only to himself. But all

that mattered was that Washington had listened to Wilde's arguments and finally decided to give him a chance, although Frost was of the opinion that the judge would've been laughed out of Congress if his reputation as a staunch Republican hadn't guaranteed him many sympathetic ears in President Hayes' government.

Still, having read through Wilde's report, the tall lawman had to admit, albeit reluctantly, that a fighting force comprised of criminals with nothing to lose could certainly be effective, if handled in the right way. They could fight their fellow outlaws on an equal footing, provided it was made worth their while, of course. They did not have to work to the letter of the law, and neither did they have to observe town, county or even state boundaries.

Fire with fire.

It wasn't such a bad idea – until you looked at the half-dozen convicts Wilde had chosen for Frost to mould into his elite force.

'Why us, marshal?'

Boone's question derailed Frost's train of thought.

'Why you?' he replied. He raked a cold gaze over them. 'Because you fight as dirty as the scum you're going to be sent up against,' he said. 'And you're not afraid to kill.'

And, he added silently, *you're expendable.*

Dark sat forward, wearing the smile of a snake. 'I ain't so sure, marshal. I played the good guy once before, and this is where it got me. But there's one thing I *do* like. See, if we're gonna fight, we'll need guns,' he remarked. 'And if we got guns, what's to stop us from shootin' *you*?'

Frost's grey eyes glittered. 'The same thing that'll keep you loyal to Judge Wilde's 'cause',' he replied tightly. 'Money.'

There was silence as the prisoners took that in. Money. A magic word. The greed it conjured up made even Longblade's depthless eyes stir briefly.

'The deal is this,' Frost went on, all business. 'You will never get a pardon from the government. The minute one of you fouls up, you *all* go back to prison. No exceptions. But each mission you undertake and complete successfully means you get to keep your freedom just a *little* while longer.'

Dark spat on the plank floor. 'What kind of a deal is that?'

'Not a bad one, considering the alternative.'

'But this ain't freedom.'

'No, but if you guys do like I say, it won't always be like this.'

Dark sat back. 'Tell us about the money,' he said.

Frost did.

'Any rewards you claim during the course of a mission will be paid up straight away and split six ways. You …'

'Hey, hold on there, marshal!'

Frost paused. 'Go ahead, Forrest.'

The big, bearded man scowled. 'Listen, I don't kill a man unless he's got it comin',' he said. 'But if I *do* kill some owlhoot, I sure as hell don't intend to share the reward with the rest of these no-hopers.'

'That's tough,' Frost decided. 'But you'll do like I say. All of you will, unless you want to go back to the Pen. And don't forget, some rewards only get paid out if the gent in question is still breathing, so don't get too trigger-happy.'

Frost sensed unrest in the men.

'And anyway,' he added.

'Yeah?'

'Apart from the reward money, there's something else to consider,' he went on. 'It would take an ordinary lawman a lot of hours, and consequently a lot of money, to track down and fight the kind of outlaws you're going up against. That's why the government has agreed to pay you every time you put your miserable hides on the line.'

'How much?' Chance asked bluntly. He was still in his late twenties, but his hazel eyes were the eyes of a much older man, and the rest of his features were carved in rough, slightly sad lines.

Frost held back a moment before replying, then said, 'A thousand dollars for every job you undertake successfully.'

'A thousand dollars *each*?'

'Each.'

There was a moment of complete, stunned silence. Then a couple of the men sighed. A couple more whistled as if they couldn't believe their luck.

Frost stood before the blackboard, pleased with

the reaction, because it meant that they hadn't stopped to wonder why Washington had been so ready to agree to such an incredible payroll.

Because they didn't expect the men to come back from their first mission in order to collect.

'They must be some jobs you got planned, marshal,' said Boone.

'They are.'

'So when do we start?' asked McCord.

'That hasn't been decided yet.'

'Well, where in hell are we?' asked Dark. 'You decided *that* yet?'

'Sure. We're about fifty miles east of Yuma,' Frost replied. 'Army built this place slap-bang in the middle of nowhere, then decided they didn't need it. So from now on, it's ours. And if any of you boys *still* don't feel at home,' he added, smiling without warmth, 'think twice before you try to escape. There's fifty miles of desert in every direction. You guys'd never make it.'

The men digested that in silence.

'All right, that's it for now,' Frost concluded with a sigh. 'Jellicoe, this place could use a little work. Take three men to check and repair the roofs of the barracks, messhall and officers' quarters.'

'Yo!'

'Mason, take the rest over to the livery and corral. I've got some horses coming in later today, so make sure any repairs that need carrying out get done. Got that?'

Both guards nodded.
'So do it!' Frost barked.
They did.

Four

Frost's horses arrived in a boiling cloud of dust around three o'clock that afternoon. The drum-roll of hooves began as a distant rumble and grew until the prisoners, now slippery with sweat from the day-long repair work, straightened aching backs to see what was happening.

Dark, McCord and Longblade, who'd drawn roof-repair duty, saw them first, crossing the yellow, sun-cracked desert floor by way of a barely discernible wagon trace that wound toward the outpost from the north.

'Eight ... no, ten horses,' McCord said, almost to himself.

'Eleven,' said Longblade. It was the first thing he'd said outside his Apache tongue since the six men had been herded together fifteen hours before.

McCord glanced at him, then narrowed his pale blue eyes. Eleven. The half-breed was right, but only because McCord hadn't bothered to include the wrangler, who was chasing the horses up from the rear. Still, no matter. As they came nearer, the three men and Jellicoe, who was keeping an eye, and a shotgun barrel, on them, picked out the sleek, sturdy forms of the animals; a mixture of duns and bays and paints, with thick, black manes flying wild along muscular, glistening necks. Good stock, McCord decided, horses that could take up and maintain any mile-eating pace and probably run until their hearts burst if the situation demanded it.

Dark, however, was not held captive by the approaching tide of horse-flesh. Unlike McCord and Longblade, he had never felt such a love of horses that he had tried his hand at stealing them. To him, a horse was simply a thing to be used. So long as it got you where you were going, you were all right. And anyway, the albino had more pressing matters to consider.

He studied the surrounding terrain through shrewd, slitted eyes. Harsh, dry and desolate, it stretched in every direction until it lost itself in the shimmering distance. Thoughtfully he wet his lips.

At night a man without possibles would freeze out there. By day the sun would set his brains to bubbling. Unless he knew what he was about, he would find nothing upon which to survive in that wilderness. Fifty miles might just as well be fifty thousand.

But Nathan Dark *did* know what he was about. He was nothing if not a survivor.

Still, it was chancy. *Damn* chancy.

Just below him, Abel Frost came out of the

officers' quarters and hurried across the parade
ground toward the outpost's two bolted gates.
Dark watched him move. How old was he, forty,
forty-five? Something like that. Dark wondered if
he was as tough as he looked, decided he probably
was.

Just supposing, he thought. Just supposing I
found a way to slip my chains and bust out of
here?

Frost would come after him, he was sure. And
since Dark would most likely be a-foot and Frost
mounted, what would happen when the marshal
caught up with him?

Good question, he thought, deciding: *I'll need a
gun or a knife.*

Now Mason was herding Chance, Boone and
Forrest out of the corral, where they had been
patching up those parts of the adobe wall that had
crumbled in the dry desert air and caved in. Dark
looked at them, recalling the words Forrest had
used earlier to sum them up. No-hopers, he'd said.
And he was right, the big ugly bastard. They were
all no-hopers except for him. Because one way or
another, Nathan Dark was getting out of there.

With an effort, Frost hauled back the thick
wooden bar that pinned the outpost gates shut,
and began to drag them open one at a time. The
screech of dry hinges tore through the hot
afternoon air. Almost before he had finished, the
horses flooded into the compound with a sound
like cannon-fire, and dust bubbled up around
them. Instinctively, the men on the ground began

to wave their arms and yell and whistle to guide the animals into the newly-overhauled corral. Then Boone went forward into their dust and swung the five-bar gate shut behind them.

Didn't take 'em long to get you well-trained, did it? Dark thought, and spat. Then he, and all the others, turned their attention to the newcomer who had brought the horses in.

The man slipped down from his McClellan with a grace that belied his form, because he was short and fiftyish, with a big belly and thick, stubby legs. He was dressed in a mixture of store-bought clothes and old Army blues. His face was red and craggy. His eyes were like two holes poked into dough, with just a hint of twinkling green peeking from their depths. His nose was a much-broken lump in the centre of his face and his mouth was a thick-lipped, twisted slash. He took off a battered old kepi, revealing white hair shaved close to his skull, and batted the hat against one leg to loosen some of the dust that still clung to it. He didn't have a neck; his squarish head seemed to rise up out of his wide shoulders like a hard, jagged rock.

He looked like one hard, mean sonofabitch.

Frost finished closing the gates and re-crossed the parade. When he was close enough to the newcomer, he reached out to clap him on one shoulder.

'You made it back all right, then?' Frost asked.

'Sure, and didn't I always?'

'Any trouble?'

'No.'

The wrangler set his kepi back atop his head and glanced from Chance, Boone and Forrest, nearby, to Dark, McCord and Longblade, still up on the messhall roof. He said, 'These are the fellers, are they?'

'They are.'

'Oooh boy. Looks like you got your work cut out for you this time, Abel.'

'*We*, you mean.'

'Who're you?' Dark called down.

As the newcomer narrowed his eyes in Dark's direction, Frost made the introductions. 'Boys, this here's T T O'Connor, the best NCO the Army ever had. If I was you, I'd get to love him, 'cause from now on he's gonna be the closest thing you'll ever get to a mother.'

O'Connor gave a little bow.

Chance frowned. 'What's that mean? What you doin' way out here, O'Connor?'

The NCO's eyes twinkled. 'You'll find out,' he replied. His gentle Irish brogue seemed to belie his tough-as-knuckles appearance, but Chance wasn't fooled for a moment. This man was hard. Maybe the hardest.

'All right, you two,' Frost said to Jellicoe and Mason. 'Get 'em back to work.' Immediately the men began to complain. Ignoring them, the lawman again directed his attention to O'Connor, obviously pleased to see him. 'Didn't get much of a chance to talk last night, T T, but I'm thinking we'd better have words. Put up your horse and come over to my quarters, all right?'

O'Connor nodded and led his bay towards the stable.

Fifteen minutes later Frost heard a light rap on his door and told the burly NCO to come in. O'Connor did so, tossing his old cap in one corner and glancing around the room. It was about twelve feet square, the same chocolate brown of the ante-room in the admin block, neat and orderly but lacking any warmth whatsoever. It was a man's room, and O'Connor immediately felt at home in it.

'Help yourself,' Frost said, indicating a bottle of Forty Rod and a spare glass on the small table beneath the room's only window.

O'Connor did as he was invited. 'Give you a refill?'

Frost held out his own glass. 'Sure.'

Even though the window was part-way open, the room was still oven-hot. Sounds of the men at work and bitching came through the afternoon air. O'Connor filled Frost's glass, then sank into a chair by the door. 'Good luck.'

'Long life.'

They drank.

Frost had first met O'Connor during his time with the Fourteenth Infantry, when he had fought alongside General Crook against the Paiutes out in Idaho Territory. Sergeant Timothy Thomas O'Connor had been the 14th's fixer; a fighter and career soldier who knew no other life than that of war. He was fiercely loyal to his friends and hell-on-earth to his enemies. Luckily he counted Frost among his friends.

It was fortunate to Frost's way of thinking that T T had been available to help out in his latest assignment, and he had a shrewd notion that if pressed, O'Connor would agree, because when the NCO's last hitch had finished three months earlier, he had suddenly realised that at fifty-four he was too old to re-up again. The future *could* have been bleak for a man who knew only how to fight. But at the moment, O'Connor thought it looked downright rosy.

'What have you got on these six fellers you're so fond of?' the NCO asked, indicating the outpost beyond the window. 'These Wilde boys of yours?'

Frost gave in to a quirky smile. 'Well, Dark's the one to watch out for,' he said at once.

'The white-face?'

'Yeah.' He reached under his cot and drew out a satchel from which he took six manilla folders. He sorted through them until he came to the one marked with the albino's name.

Nathan Dark had been born in El Paso, Texas, sometime in December 1844. He'd grown up in an orphanage, run away at the age of twelve and promptly fallen into bad company. Although he'd turned up in the 3rd Texas Infantry during the War, his military service was hardly distinguished. In fact, he was caught and busted three times for grave-robbing and selling medical supplies to the enemy.

After the War, he spent a few months hunting bounty on some of the hardcases left over from Appomattox. When that dried up he tried his hand at stagecoach robbery, buffalo hunting and whiskey peddling. In 1878 he turned up in New Mexico as a gun-for-hire during the Lincoln County War. He grew pretty tight with Billy Bonney around that time, too.

'No wonder he ended up in the Yuma Pen,' said O'Connor.

'Right,' Frost agreed. 'But here's the interesting part. When we got Dark, he was doing time for killing the president of the McNary and Springerville Savings Trust, feller named Hatch. Seems Hatch refused to pay out on a reward that Dark was within his rights to collect.'

'Huh?'

'Dark retrieved eight thousand dollars that had been stolen from the bank's branch in Trenton. Came across it by accident when he caught up with and killed Cherokee Pete Parker, the sonofabitch who'd carried out the job a fortnight before. Well, for once in his life Dark decided to do the decent thing. He handed the money in, figuring to earn eight hundred dollars the legal way.'

'What happened?' O'Connor asked.

'Hatch, the president of the bank, took one look at him and refused to pay him his reward. Even went so far as to suggest that Dark'd been in cahoots with Parker all along, and that they'd had some kind of falling out among thieves. There was an argument, then a struggle. Maybe the banker went for a gun, I don't know. Anyhow, Dark shot him twice, then grabbed up the money and ran smack into the local law. Right now he should be serving fifteen at hard labour.'

O'Connor nodded. 'I'll keep an eye on him,' he decided. 'Go on.'

Tom Boone, the negro, was next. Born September 21 1845 in Macon, Louisiana, he'd worked as foreman of a tobacco plantation up until two years before. He'd had a wife, two children, a decent home and good prospects. The only time he'd ever fired a gun was during the War, when he'd joined the *Corps D'Afrique* at the age of seventeen.

'So what went wrong?' asked the NCO.

Frost shrugged. 'We're not sure and he won't say,' he replied. 'But something bad happened that cost him his family and his future. He's been a drifter these last couple of years, and for the most part he's kept out of trouble. But about eighteen months ago he picked up with Nick Ordinans. That's where he learned how to handle a gun.'

O'Connor finished his whiskey. 'We talkin' about *the* Nick Ordinans?' he asked. 'The man they say was the fastest of 'em all? The one as got himself kilt in Phoenix a month or so back?'

Frost nodded. A small-time gunman named Travis had spotted Ordinans down at the Crystal Palace, and seeing a chance to increase his reputation, called him out. There was a gunfight and Travis won.

'So how does Boone figure in it?'

'Travis killed Ordinans. Boone killed Travis.'

O'Connor raised his eyebrows. 'Fair fight?'

'Not according to Travis's cronies. That's why Boone was arrested and sentenced to hang ten days from now.'

'How about according to some independent witnesses?'

Frost was careful to keep his expression neutral. 'Fair fight,' he said quietly.

Silence thickened in the room as O'Connor glanced out the window, figuring the implications. 'If that's true,' he muttered. 'If Boone was faster than the man who killed the *fastest* ...'

Frost nodded, thinking of the quiet and largely inoffensive black member of the team. 'Right,' he replied. 'Boone must be the fastest of them all.'

They came for Pancho, as Pancho knew they must, at noon of that same day, just as the little Mexican finished burying the unfortunate bounty hunters Cole and Vincent in a shallow dip of sand and scrub some distance from Tacalima.

He had just started the tiring journey back to his miserable cantina, still leaking sweat from his exertions, when he heard the thunder of their approaching horses, and paused. He had hoped it was just his ageing blood pumping in his ears.

It wasn't.

As he squinted off to the west, almost afraid to look, he saw them about a kilometre away and closing fast. Five riders; the Black Wolf's men.

Pancho stood rooted to the dry, lifeless earth, his old spade clutched between his nerveless fingers. At first he had hoped that the Black Wolf and *Senor* Jarvis would not connect him with the bounty hunters. And indeed, why should they? After the killing, as the two outlaws made ready to leave the cantina with its smell of fresh death fouling the heated air, Pancho had almost fallen over himself to express his shock and horror and most of all his complete *surprise* that such an outrage should befall his two most honoured patrons.

The two outlaws had told him not to worry about it, that such sudden violence was something to be expected in their line of work, that it was the kind of thing that could have happened to them at any time, what the Black Wolf himself called an occupational hazard.

But somewhere at the back of his mind, Pancho knew that sooner or later, the outlaws would wonder how Cole and Vincent knew where to find them, and start asking questions. For Pancho, *awkward* questions.

Starting now.

When they were near enough, the five riders reined in sharply, showering Pancho with dust and forming a confining wall of horse-flesh around him. Sweat coursed down his face. It dripped off his nose and chin and slipped down his narrow chest. He was a small man; it was an effort to look up into the hard, compassionless faces that surrounded him.

Three of the men were white, the other two black. They were all heavily armed. They returned Pancho's stare with flat, cruel eyes that gave no indication of their business with him this hot day out in the cholla-choked desert a quarter-mile from town.

Finally the Mexican's eyes settled on Will Slade, whose rangy frame was forked across a sturdy sorrel gelding. Slade was the Black Wolfe's *segundo*; he kept the rest of the men in line when the Wolf and Jarvis were otherwise occupied.

'*Buenos dias, Señor* Slade. *Como esta usted?* You are ... you are well today?'

Slade did not reply. He was around the mid-thirties and his long thin face carried a heavy tan and many lines. His eyes were as blue and cold as ice and his mouth was twisted in a contemptuous sneer. He was a man who did not smile often. When he did smile, a wise man could tell it meant trouble.

He smiled now.

'Been out huntin' buried treasure, Pancho?'

The Mexican stared up at him for a pair of heartbeats, then glanced down at the spade in his white-knuckled grip. When he realised that the *norteamericano* was joking, Pancho's giggle escaped high and nervous and verging on hysteria. 'I ... No, no, I ... ' He indicated the way he had just come. 'The bounty hunters ... I was ... I buried them.'

'Oh yeah,' Slade replied in his quiet, disarming tone. 'The bounty hunters.'

Pancho pawed sweat out of his eyes and bobbed his head.

'The Wolf'd 'preciate a word with you 'bout them bounty hunters,' Slade went on. 'Now.' He indicated one of the two negroes, who sat aboard a restless dun. 'You c'n ride double with Bohannan here.'

Pancho did not move. He was transfixed by a sudden vision of fangs, eyes and death. The Black Wolf's chipped and broken teeth. The madman-bright eyes of Crazy Bob Jarvis. And *his* death. Pancho's death. He threw his shovel into the sand.

But he didn't know that for sure. There might still be a way to avoid so unpleasant and permanent an end to his attempted treachery. If he was clever. If he could find a way out.

He shuffled towards Bohannan and clambered awkwardly up into the saddle behind him. Only then did Slade move, wheeling his sorrel, jamming his spurs into its flanks and setting off back west, towards the disused monastery from whence they had come.

The other men followed at a gallop and Pancho clung desperately to Bohannan's thick waist, trying to ignore the taste of bile rising to his dry lips.

The monastery was surrounded by four tile-topped adobe walls that stretched into a hundred and fifty foot square atop the sage-grey rise overlooking the town. As the riders approached, a man in the watch-tower above the rough-hewn oak gates called down to someone beyond the wall. A moment later, the great portals began to swing open.

Hanging on to Bohannan's belt for all he was worth, Pancho eyed the looming structure with more than a little trepidation. It had been built in 1768 by a monastic order that had been greatly disappointed when Tacalima failed to flourish as they had expected. When an outbreak of smallpox virtually wiped out the coarse-robed monks six years later, no-one had been sent to replace them. The monastery had been allowed to die a gradual, crumbling death. Now it was a ruin, but a strong and easily-defended one, which was why the Black Wolf had chosen it as his refuge from the American authorities half a year earlier.

Pancho squeezed his eyes shut against the sweat coursing down his forehead. He was forty-three years of age; he felt much older. In truth, he felt like fainting. But he knew that even in unconsciousness there was no escape from *El Lobo Negro*.

As soon as they passed through the gates, the riders brought their horses to a stiff-legged, skidding halt. Pancho opened his eyes to find himself in a courtyard. Two men slowly closed the gates behind him. He slipped down from the spirited dun and Slade and the others spurred their mounts toward a shady stable to the northwest.

Pancho looked around him. He had never been inside the monastery before. Not even as an inquisitive child had he trudged up the hill to explore it. There was a surprisingly ornate and equally functional fountain in the centre of the yard, and beyond that what had once been the monks' cells. A long, off-white adobe building that he took to have been the monks' place of worship stood directly opposite, its old, now peeling entranceway almost hidden beneath the shadows of a long arched porch overhang.

As they went about their business around him, the Black Wolf's men gave him curious looks, as did the painted *putas Señor* Jarvis had brought in from Camenez to keep them happy. They seemed to find his discomfort amusing. They also seemed to be busy. There was tension in the air that Pancho was certain had nothing to do with him.

'Pancho.'

The little Mexican jumped and turned to find Bob Jarvis standing right beside him, a crooked smile hanging from his otherwise lifeless face. The consumptive killer had approached him with all the silence of a thought.

'Follow me.'

Without waiting to make sure Pancho did just that, Jarvis turned and disappeared into the main building. Inside, away from the glare of the mid-day sun, it was cooler. Crazy Bob made little noise moving down the corridor. Pancho hurried to catch him up.

Again Pancho cursed himself for a fool. If only he'd known how his 'partnership' with the two Sonoita-based bounty hunters would end. But he hadn't stopped to give the matter much thought. His thinking had been clouded by the reward money.

At last they stepped into a large, high-ceilinged room that held many echoes. Sunlight streamed in through three tall, cracked windows to splash across a long, scarred dining table and bounce off the plain white walls.

The Black Wolf was sitting at the head of the table, his massive bulk dwarfing an otherwise impressive button-studded chair. He grinned when his bloodshot eyes settled on Pancho, and the cantina owner shivered.

'Ah, Pancho. Come on in here,' the Wolf said sociably.

As Pancho did as he was told, the big black outlaw got to his feet, stretching out to his full six feet six inches. Sunlight spilled off the cartridges in the bandolier across his chest as he came forward to tower above the Mexican. Floorboards creaked beneath his giant tread. Bob Jarvis swaggered across to sit on the edge of the table to watch whatever was about to take place.

The Wolf bent to peer into Pancho's face. 'What's up, Pancho? Somethin' troublin' you? You look sick.'

The little Mexican shook his head. 'I … It is a headache, *señor*. A headache is all.'

The Wolf nodded his understanding, and Pancho felt his gut beginning to unclench. Maybe things would be all right after all.

'I'll make this quick, then,' the negro said in his rumbling voice. 'Seein' as how you got a headache, an' me an' the boys got places to go.'

Again Pancho nodded his balding head, peering

enquiringly up at the outlaw. '*Si Señor*?'

'*Si*. I only got the one thing to say anyhow.'

'*Si, sēnor*?'

The outlaw nodded. Then his eyes went dull and heavy-lidded. 'You shouldn't oughta've done it, Pancho.'

He grabbed the back of Pancho's head in his massive right palm, whipped out his Colt Wells Fargo and jammed the cold muzzle up against the Mexican's lower abdomen. Their eyes locked for a split second before the Black Wolf fired three bullets in quick succession and Pancho jerked violently as his guts spilled out of his back like thick red ropes.

Half a minute later Will Slade appeared in the doorway. He saw what was left of Pancho splashed across the tiled floor and smiled.

'Send him home an' tell his *amigos* why I done it,' the negro rumbled. 'Just in case they try pullin' the same stunt.'

'Got it.'

'An' make sure the boys're ready to pull out in an hour.'

Slade's eyes flared in anticipation. 'It's still on then?' he said. 'The Army payroll?'

The Wolf nodded. 'It's still on,' he replied. 'It sure as hell is.'

Little over an hour later the Wolf, Jarvis, Slade and twelve other hardcases rode out through the monastery gates and kicked their horses into a steady gallop northeast. The people of Tacalima, already spooked by having Pancho's bloody carcass dumped in the middle of their only street, crossed themselves as they watched them go.

Five

At sundown, with the repair work more or less completed, the six convicts were marched across to the bath-house and told to wash down. Grimy with sweat, they didn't need telling twice.

Twenty minutes later they were marched back across to the messhall, where Mason dished up six bowls of watery, just about meatless stew. The men ate in silence, too tired even to bitch about the food. They managed to kick up a racket cleaning the dishes afterward, though.

Jellicoe and Mason herded them back into the barracks just as the Arizona sky began to streak with crimson, then hand-cuffed each man to his bunk, blew out the room's single lamp, locked the door, bolted the shutters and left them alone. It was just after seven-thirty in the evening.

Dark lay back in the shadows, considering his escape. There was an old, twisted nail in his pants' pocket that he had managed to secrete there whilst working up on the roof. With that nail between his long white fingers it would be less than a minute's work to unlock the cuffs that bound him to the bunk. He could probably get rid of those Goddamn ankle-chains, too.

But instead of going to work on the manacles straight away, he just lay where he was, listening to the heavy, measured breathing of the other men, waiting for them to fall asleep. He knew he couldn't risk them discovering his escape attempt. He knew they would remember Frost's warning that if one of them fouled up, they would *all* go back to the Pen. He knew they would find a way to stop him.

But Nathan Dark wasn't going to be stopped. He would just lay back and relax, bide his time, choose his moment.

Around him the other men stirred, trying to get comfortable. The albino listened to them, refusing to give in to his own fatigue.

No hopers, he thought. *No hopers, the …*

Suddenly he stiffened. Around him he felt the other men tense up, too, all except for Forrest, that was, who was already snoring.

'Hear that?' McCord said softly.

'What; Forrest drivin' the cows home?'

'Very funny. No, outside. Hear it?'

Dark grunted. Yeah, he heard it. Voices. Too far off to make out what was being said. Then the now-familiar screech of dry hinges as the gates were opened. The clatter of a team of horses, the jingle-rattle-creak of harness and spring. A wagon.

The men strained to hear what was happening outside. Forrest carried on snoring.

'Visitors?' Chance asked through the darkness.

'Someone bringin' in supplies, maybe?' suggested Boone.

They continued to listen, picking out odd words here and there. Then they heard one word clearer than the rest, a name, and each man felt a sudden charge of curiosity and strangely, apprehension.

'So he's here,' said Chance.

'Huh?' asked Forrest, waking up. 'Who's here?'

'The judge,' McCord replied. 'Wilde. The guy who dreamed this whole deal up.'

The man who climbed down from the dusty buggy was small, thin and seventy. His plain grey suit clung to his spare frame and his wide-brimmed black hat sat straight atop his balding head. In the poor evening light his skin looked the dry yellow colour of old parchment.

His blue eyes were young and alive, though, within their slack pouches, and when they lit upon Marshal Frost, the old man shed years with a smile and extended his right hand.

'Frost! Good to see you again. How goes the battle?'

As they shook, Frost forced a smile, wondering what Wilde was doing back from Tucson so soon. 'All uphill, judge,' he replied. 'Mason; see to the buggy, will you?'

'Yo!'

'Judge, I'd like to have you meet Sergeant O'Connor.'

T T who had been standing just behind Frost,

stepped forward and shook with Wilde. 'Pleasure to meet ya, sir.'

'Likewise, sergeant, likewise. You've met the men?'

'Sort of.'

'And what do you think?'

O'Connor's eyes met Frost's, then returned to the judge's hollow face. 'Well,' he began awkwardly.

'Daddy!'

'Elizabeth!'

The three men turned just as the auburn-haired woman Dark had tried to approach earlier that day came hurrying across the parade to throw her arms around the old man, her plain but appealing features blurred slightly by the rapidly approaching darkness.

'Daddy! What brings you back so soon? I thought you'd be gone at least another few weeks!'

Judge Wilde returned his daughter's hug with a chuckle, then held her at arm's length. At five feet seven inches, she was taller than him, and although she was as dark as he had once been fair, she had his same lively smile and, beneath her high-necked gingham dress, his same slight build.

Father and daughter gazed at each other for several moments until O'Connor, his red face flushing even deeper with embarrassment, coughed politely and excused himself.

'Yeah, I got chores to do as well,' Frost added, shuffling his own feet. 'Besides which, I expect you want to freshen up ...'

'No, no, marshal! Although I will confess that a cup of coffee would not go amiss!'

Taking his daughter and the marshal by the arm, he led them back across the parade to what enlisted men referred to as 'officer's country'. As they approached the door to Wilde's quarters, Elizabeth hurried ahead to disappear inside and get a lamp going.

Wilde's rooms were soon bathed in a golden glow, and when Elizabeth left them to fetch coffee from the messhall, the old judge watched her fondly through a small, square window.

'You have put our little scheme to the men?' he asked without turning around.

Frost stood in the centre of the spartan room, toying with his hat. 'Yep.'

'And what did they have to say about it?'

'Not a lot. The thousand-dollars-a-job bit interested them more than anything else.'

'Hah! I thought it would.' He turned back to the marshal. He had removed his hat to reveal thin strands of grey hair swept back from a high, domed forehead. 'Sit down, marshal, sit down. We have things to discuss.'

Frost took a chair beside a chest of drawers, twisted it around and straddled it so that he could rest his folded arms on the back. It was not the kind of thing he would normally do, but there was something about Isaac Wilde that brought out belligerence in the lawman. 'I'm ready whenever you are, judge.'

The old man's eyes remained animate, although

Frost was surprised at how much he'd aged in the four or five weeks they'd known each other. In a good light Wilde looked old and tired and sick, which indeed he was. The only things that seemed to keep him going were his twenty-seven-year-old widowed daughter, Elizabeth Kelso, and this convicts-into-lawmen project, which O'Connor had nicknamed 'The Wilde Boys'.

Wilde looked down into Frost's rugged face and a smile pulled at his thin lips. 'We've got a mission, marshal,' he said quietly. 'They've given us a mission.'

He was obviously disappointed when Frost stayed where he was instead of jumping for joy. Lifting an eyebrow he enquired, 'Did you hear what I said?'

'I heard,' Frost replied. 'But I'm waiting to hear more.'

Wilde crossed to his bed and sat on the edge. 'Are you familiar with Joshua Thorne, also known as *El Lobo Negro*, the Black Wolf?'

Frost nodded. 'I've heard of him. He's a negro. Bank-robber, killer, child-fornicator.' He paused. 'Why? Are you thinking of recruiting *him*, too?'

Wilde narrowed his mouth but did not comment on Frost's sarcasm. 'You, and your men, are going after him. And one way or another, you're going to get him, too.'

Frost narrowed his grey eyes. 'Tell me more.'

'Well, you already know his reputation, so I needn't explain *why* my colleagues on Capitol Hill have chosen him as your first target. He and his partner, one 'Crazy' Bob Jarvis, are both mad-dog killers cut from the same cloth. They've raped and robbed and generally terrorised the border country long enough. Now we want them stopped.'

Frost remained impassive. He didn't know what to think, but he had the idea that this was not so much a 'mission' as a test. 'That might be easier said than done.'

'Why?'

'Because Thorne, or the Black Wolf or whatever else you want to call him, runs with a pack of about ten or fifteen *other* wolves. And in between jobs he high-tails it down to Mexico someplace, where we can't touch him.'

Wilde smiled. 'Not even if we have an invitation from President Diaz himself?' he replied.

Frost's frown asked the question.

'At the moment, our government is trying to improve relations with Mexico,' Wilde explained. 'The country is rich with silver, coal, iron, copper and dozens of other metals, so it's not difficult to understand why. And Mexico certainly wants to get its hands on a few American dollars. But there is still a lot of animosity across the border toward we *gringos*.

'In particular, the Mexican government objects to the presence of *El Lobo Negro* in their country, but since – as far as they are aware – he has committed no punishable crimes across the border, they are reluctant to send in the *federales* to flush him out.'

'So they want us to do it,' Frost said bluntly.

'As a gesture of our good will, yes,' Wilde agreed. 'You must understand that we cannot send in the Army. Negotiations are still at a very delicate stage, and any invasion of their country by a foreign force ...'

'I know,' Frost cut in sharply. 'It could be taken as a declaration of war.'

'Exactly.'

'But *El Presidente* has no objections to us using a small civilian force.'

'Our six friends across the way there, yes.'

'And me and O'Connor,' Frost added dourly.

'Yes.'

Frost thought for a while. 'Do your, uh, colleagues on Capitol Hill have any idea where we can find this Black Wolf?'

Wilde's smile broadened. He got up and crossed to a map on the wall. 'Here,' he said, pointing. 'It's little more than a jumble of shacks called Tacalima. There's an old ruin that used to be a monastery ... here. That's the Black Wolf's safe-house. That's where you'll find him.'

'You hope,' Frost said cynically.

'Oh, that's where you'll find him all right,' Wilde replied. 'The Mexican government guarantees it.'

'That's kind of 'em,' Frost muttered, studying the map.

'You're not too keen on this job, are you marshal?' Wilde asked frankly.

'No,' Frost replied without turning around. He was already estimating distances and considering strategies. 'But orders are orders. I'll get it done, or die trying. There's just a couple of things I want to make sure of.'

'Yes?'

'I don't see us being able to take the Wolf or his men alive, not all of 'em, leastways. If you'll excuse my language, bastards like that never come quietly. There'll be killing, a pitched battle, from the looks of it. I don't want your friends in Washington saying they weren't warned.'

'Don't worry. They know what kind of man this Black Wolf is, marshal, and you are authorized to deal with him in whichever way you deem best.'

Frost nodded.

'And the other thing?' Wilde asked expectantly.

The lawman grabbed up his hat in his right hand while he fingered his moustache with the left. 'On your say-so, I've promised those six cons a thousand dollars each for every job they undertake. If they come through this one, don't disappoint them.'

Wilde allowed a smile to flicker across his thin, wrinkled face as he nodded. Frost made a good leader. Although he didn't care for the men in his command, he wasn't about to see them cheated. Before the judge could reply, Elizabeth re-entered the room, carrying a tray laden with coffee pot and cups. She saw Frost making ready to leave and frowned.

'Won't you stay for coffee, marshal?'

Frost was never comfortable around women, especially those he considered handsome. That was why he'd kept his distance from this widow woman, remaining cool despite all her attempts at cordiality.

'No thank you, ma'am. I'd better get off to bed. I'm up early in the morning.' He returned his gaze to Wilde. 'I'll tell O'Connor to get supplies and ordnance prepared tonight. That way we can leave here around nine or ten tomorrow, once the men have been briefed. Suit you?'

'Admirably,' Wilde replied. He saw the lawman to the door, where he rested a thin hand on one of Frost's hard biceps. 'This is the beginning of great things for us, marshal,' he predicted. 'You might not think so right now, but I can guarantee it. You see, the law is just like a spider's web. All the little flies get stuck in it, but the big ones just crash straight on through.'

He locked eyes with the taller man.

'Starting from now, we; you, me and those men over there, we're going to make sure that justice catches up with all those big flies.'

Frost turned and opened the door without replying.

'Don't worry, marshal. I can handle Washington. You and your men will get a fair deal from me.'

'I don't doubt,' Frost agreed, stepping outside and glancing up at the night sky. 'It's whether or not I get a fair deal from the men that worries me.'

The Wolf led his men on a fairly straight line northeast across the vast, empty desert. The men sweated hard beneath the westering sun. Even

Bob Jarvis pulled out a kerchief with which to blot his skeletal face. But the Black Wolf's ebony skin remained curiously dry.

Jarvis had often wondered about that. He and the Wolf had been partners for many years, and yet not once could Jarvis recall a time when the black man had been worried by sweat.

Still, there were more important things to think about right now, as the unyielding desert floor stretched on mile after mile beneath their horses' pounding hooves. Like a forty-five hundred dollar Army payroll on its way from McKenna to Lukeville. A pay*roll* the Army would never get to pay *out*.

Come nightfall they camped in a narrow arroyo and dined on bacon, beans and cornbread. The men were in high spirits. The prospect of action always did that to them. At sun-up the following morning they rode on, still heading northeast.

Their border crossing was unremarkable. The land remained hard and dry and lonely, pin-pricked here and there by giant cacti; pinon and saguarro and prickly pear. Gradually the flat land gave way to wrinkles, the wrinkles to great distorted masses of rock and weather-smoothed boulders.

Finally the Black Wolf and his men came to a narrow body of water, rare in this thirsty stretch of Arizona, and found three nests of rocks overlooking the stream, which was called Fire-water Creek. It wound west to east beside a rutted wagon trace that led from Green's Crossing to

Lukeville. According to the Black Wolf's informant, it was along this trace that the Army payroll
would come some time that night.

The outlaws could hardly wait. ✺

As a rule, the Army allowed the Southern
Pacific to transport its money across the territory,
but just recently two payrolls had been lost to
train robbers, so the Army had decided to send its
funds by wagon with a small, and hopefully
inconspicuous guard under cover of darkness. The
route – indeed, the very *existence* – of the payroll
wagon was supposed to be a secret. But it wasn't.
And that meant that the Black Wolf would catch
the soldier-boys completely by surprise.

Each nest of rocks rose twenty to twenty-five
feet above the ground and afforded the men
hidden among them a good view of the wagon
trace. On a clear night and with a bloated moon,
the desolate land would be clear as day. Anyone
travelling the trail between those rocks would be
caught in a perfect, deadly crossfire.

Come dusk, the Wolf sent one of his best men
east along the trail to watch for the approaching
wagon. Then he and his remaining cut-throats
took up their positions among the boulders to
wait.

An hour turned into two. Dusk gave way to full
dark. The moon came out, splashing silver across
the land. Somewhere far away a wolf howled
mournfully. Nearer, one of the men yawned.
Another sneezed. Smokes were lit, enjoyed, the
butts crushed out on the cold, hard rocks. For a

long while the only sound was the waters of
Firewater Creek trickling sluggishly by.

And then,

The Black Wolf's bloodshot eyes picked out the
movement of an approaching shadow down beside
the trail. All at once there was electricity in the
air. Phil Ridley, the man the Wolf had sent out
ahead, crabbed into view, disappeared again, then
suddenly materialised at the black outlaw's side.

'They're comin',' he said in a sharp whisper. He
had a long, weathered face and a pencil-line
moustache. 'Be here in about fifteen minutes.'

'How many?'

'Nine, all told. Two up on the wagon, six ridin'
shotgun, an' a lieutenant.'

The Black Wolf nodded. Just like his informant
had told him. He dismissed Ridley and closed his
grip around the old Henry repeater he favoured.
In the tower of rocks opposite, Bob Jarvis' thin
mouth twitched in anticipation. Pay-day was
coming.

Just over a quarter-hour later they heard the
rumbling rattle of the approaching wagon. One
stretched minute after that they saw it about fifty
yards away, following the trace in from the east.
Two men sat atop the swaying seat, one handling
the reins, the other cradling a Springfield rifle in
his lap. A fresh-faced lieutenant led the way and
his six troopers came after him, riding their
regulation bays in three ranks of double file.

The Black Wolf sighted along the blued steel
barrel and closed one eye as he took aim.

The payroll wagon and its unsuspecting guard came nearer.

Jarvis' eyes lit up expectantly. Around him the other outlaws were tensed for action.

The Black Wolf tightened one thick finger on the trigger.

The soldiers rode nearer and nearer ...

The Black Wolf fired.

The report cracked through the nighttime stillness and the Springfield-carrying guard on the wagon seat stood up, screamed and fell back onto the roped-down tarpaulin that covered the wagon's contents, spraying blood in a wide arc.

A lot of things happened very quickly then. The driver reflexively stepped on the brake, bringing the wagon to a slurring halt. The lieutenant and his men fought to control their panicky horses and drag their sidearms out at the same time. Bob Jarvis came up straight and sent a bullet into the wagon driver's head, spilling him off the wagon into the creek. A couple of soldiers got off hasty, poorly-aimed shots. A volley of returned fire knocked two of them out of their saddles and killed three horses.

Thrown into the sand beside the trail, the young lieutenant rolled, came up on his knees, tore his Cavalry Colt from its flap-down holster and triggered five shots into the high ground opposite. He was pleased to hear a strange coughing scream and then see a body tumble from the rocks to splash into the creek.

But his pleasure was short-lived. Another of his

men, a nineteen-year-old named Simmons, took a
bullet in the upper chest and fell onto his back,
fingers digging at the wound and legs kicking
spasmodically.

The young lieutenant's face turned pale. It was
suicide to continue fighting against unknown
odds. He couldn't put his men at risk any longer.
He wouldn't. Before he realised what he was
doing, he yelled, '*Hold your fire! Hold your fire up
there!*'

Abruptly the night fell silent, and the silence
was the weird, unbroken silence of a tomb. The
lieutenant looked around him with eyes unused to
battle. The trace was littered with the bodies of
men and animals. Only three other soldiers were
still on their feet, and two of those were wounded.
The two horses hitched to the wagon stamped and
shifted nervously. The other horses still alive had
bolted during the fiercest fighting.

'Good thinkin', soldier boy,' said a deep voice
from somewhere above and to his right. 'Toss your
guns away.'

The lieutenant glanced into the beaten, shocked
faces of his men. Of what was left of his men. They
all threw their guns into the sand.

The rocks came alive then, as the outlaws
climbed down from their vantage points like
fourteen gigantic ants. While some dragged the
bodies of horses and men off the trail, clearing the
way ahead, two others moved to the payroll
wagon, quieting the horses and rolling the dead
guard off the tarpaulin.

The four soldiers watched them through blurred eyes. Reaction was starting to set in. The lieutenant could feel his hands trembling.

Finally they were herded together by Will Slade and a couple of other hardcases and told to turn around and stretch out on their stomachs. One of the troopers, expecting a bullet in the back, told Slade to go to hell and made a lunge for him. Slade's .36 calibre Navy Starr appeared in his fist, roared once, then returned to leather. The trooper yelped, buckled, clutched his stomach and collapsed.

The three survivors did as they were told.

Five long minutes dragged by, with the soldiers preparing themselves for the worst. They heard the familiar sound of the payroll wagon rattling away, then the drumming of many horses pounding after it. By that time the young lieutenant was trembling all over.

They lay face-down in the sand for ten more minutes, listening to Firewater Creek gurgling through the night. When they could stand the suspense no longer they rolled over, keeping their movements slow and cautious.

They glanced around the scene of the massacre.

Apart from the remains of the dead, they were alone. The bandits had melted off into the midnight gloom.

Abruptly the lieutenant stopped trembling. All he felt now was humiliation and the heavy weight of responsibility to his men. His poor, dead men. He sat up, got his feet under him and pushed himself erect. When his two men joined him, they saw in his eyes a much older man.

'They'll pay,' said the lieutenant, whose name was Warren Baxter. He stumbled away from the others, searching for his Colt and a Springfield. 'I'm going to make sure of that.'

One of the troopers, who, at the age of twenty was only three years younger than the lieutenant, wiped a hand across his battle-smudged face. 'Sir. Maybe we'd better get to Lukeville first and ...'

But Lieutenant Baxter was not listening. He continued his search, muttering over and over again, 'They'll pay, all right. I personally guarantee it.'

Six

The prospect of going after the Black Wolf left Deputy US Marshal Abel Frost feeling none of the sensations he normally associated with setting out on a new manhunt. There was no sense of excitement or anticipation to start the blood singing in his veins, not even a faint quiver of fear that this time 'round the luck that had seen him through so many do-or-die assignments might finally give out.

All he felt now was a sinking, slightly depressed feeling that left him quiet and dispirited; nothing to do with having to lock horns with such a notorious killer, but everything to do with the company he'd be keeping whilst he got the job done.

Dark, Boone, Chance, Longblade, Forrest and McCord.

The Wilde boys.

Christ.

That sinking feeling stayed with Frost all the next day, beginning the moment he woke up and continuing right through the briefing and Judge

Wilde's subsequent pep-talk to the men, who seemed to view him as a crazy old coot it was probably wisest to humour. T T got things organised; the men had their ankle-chains removed and bitched about the kind of clothes that had been chosen for them, the horses they were given and generally about having to ride a hundred miles and chew Christ knew how much Mexican dust just to settle some black outlaw's hash. ◦

As Frost climbed aboard his appaloosa, Jellicoe and Mason wished him good luck, as did the judge and his daughter, Elizabeth Kelso. Frost had the awful feeling he was going to need it. He rode out with the six convicts strung out behind him and O'Connor bringing up the rear.

The going was tough but the progress was good. They nooned beneath the shade of a granite bluff in a dry wash twenty-some miles to the south and dined on corned beef and coffee. Afterwards, O'Connor rested his back up against the rock wall beside Frost, took a sip of coffee and swilled it around his mouth to shift some of the dust from his teeth. Some little distance away the men searched around for some shade in which to rest bones unused to riding.

Dark's voice drifted on the muggy afternoon air. 'Hey, O'Connor, how 'bout openin' up some more of that beef, huh? And maybe some peaches?'

O'Connor swatted at a buzzing fly. 'Shuddup.'

'But hell, I got my stomach through to my backbone here!'

'Why don't you try chewin' on your tongue fer a while?' suggested Forrest.

'Yeah,' McCord agreed. 'Try chewing it and then swallowing it.'

Dark dismissed them with a sharp movement of his pale right hand. 'Ah, the hell with you guys.' He settled in the shade some way off.

The grizzled NCO cast a glance at Frost and saw the distant glaze to his eyes. 'Somethin' ailin' you, Abel?' he asked quietly. 'You're sittin' around with a face as long as Sunday.'

The lawman blinked, then smiled wistfully. 'It's nothing.'

'Spill it, boy. Don't let it fester inside you.'

But how could Frost give voice to his suspicions about the Tucson office only giving him this job because they thought he was too old to handle anything else? 'It's nothing,' he said again. 'Just thinking about these sorry sonsofbitches we've gotta work with.'

O'Connor allowed himself a good-natured smile as he returned his gaze to the six convicts.

'Funny thing about the human race,' he remarked casually. 'No matter how many folks get dragged into the world, you never come across the same kind twice. You take ten men, or twenty, hell, take a hundred. I can guarantee you won't get any two alike. That's why you got to handle each one a different way. Now, you take these six characters here ...'

Frost watched O'Connor's profile closely. 'Yeah?'

'Fellers like them, it's not that they're so tough or stubborn or obstinate. They're just plain *ornery*. Give 'em a direct order and they'll do anything they can to disobey it. So if you want anything out'n' em, you've got to do it crafty-like.'

Frost fingered his moustache. 'Will you get to the point?'

'Sure I'll get to the point. If you're gonna get anywhere with these buckos, you're gonna have to bend a little, Abel. Come down to their level a bit and ...'

'Oh no. The only thing these bastards respect is strength ...'

The NCO raised his shaggy eyebrows. 'You reckon? I'm not so sure. You watch this.'

He got up and crossed the flat, dusty earth to one of the two pack-horses, where he rummaged in a pannier for a moment, then turned to the six convicts, paying special attention to the Apache half-breed, Sam Longblade.

'Hey, you guys. I hate to say it, but maybe Dark's right. That corned beef, hell, all it was was salt and fat. How'd you like some *real* vittles?'

The six prisoners watched O'Connor suspiciously.

'Reckon you could find some game around here, Longblade? Coupl'a rabbits, maybe?'

The Apache neither moved nor spoke. He just stared at O'Connor from out of a flat, coppery face with high cheekbones and a thin, unhappy mouth.

From his blind side, T T produced the item he'd taken from the pack-horse, a hunter's Bowie knife with a ten-inch blade and a coffin-shaped handle. The sight of it made the half-breed's eyes widen. Up until he'd been thrown in prison it had been his prize possession. He had thought never to see it again.

O'Connor approached the young buck and offered him the knife, handle first. 'Go see what you can scare up, will ya?'

Still the Apache sat immobile, although his eyes remained fixed on the blade. After another few seconds he reached out, took the knife and got soundlessly to his feet. Without a word he moved off along the dry wash and soon disappeared from sight.

'You *do* know,' said Dark irritably, 'that you ain't never gonna see that redskin again?'

'Not 'til he comes back to shove that knife in your ribs,' added Chance.

'Quit bellyachin',' O'Connor replied, apparently unconcerned. He returned to Frost, sat down beside him and finished his coffee.

'But *Jesus*, sarge!' said McCord.

'He'll be back,' replied T T.

'I hope to Christ you're right,' Frost muttered angrily.

'I am,' O'Connor said confidently. 'Y'see, it's all a matter of *respect*. Self-respect. And that's what I gave that half-blood just now.'

Frost just cursed and stared off across the shimmering plain.

'Abel,' O'Connor said with a chuckle. 'You're a damn' fine lawman and your arrest rate is second to none. But you don't know shit about people, boy. You really don't.'

Longblade had been born in an Indian camp along the Salt River sometime around 1853. A wild, quick-tempered youth, his fiery temperament had always been held in check by the calming influence of his mother, a Scotswoman who had come to nurse the tribe through a cholera epidemic some years before and stayed on to adopt a whole new way of life. When she died of pneumonia in 1871, the teenager's life had become a never-ending mixture of tribal warfare, horse-stealing, hard drinking and harder loving.

Until one summer's day when many soldiers came to the camp of the White Mountain Apaches. They said they were looking for some settlers the Indians had taken captive, and the Apaches were happy to watch them search, knowing that no *pinda-lik-oyi* would be found in camp because Longblade's people never took prisoners.

There was one among the long-knives who was young and nervous, however. He was new to the west and unused to Indians. He was standing three feet away from Longblade's father when the Apache moved suddenly to ease a cramp. The soldier panicked and fired his Springfield. The .45/50 bullet shattered the Indian's left hip, leaving him crippled, useless and old before his time. Because of awkward internal injuries, he died three months later.

Longblade was overcome by grief. Suddenly all

he craved was revenge against the whites. He joined the Mimbreno renegade Geronimo, gouging a scar of terror along the border with a series of lightning guerrilla raids. Soon he became one of Geronimo's most trusted lieutenants.

But as each new outrage became bloodier than the last, so Longblade's acts of violence became mechanical and without purpose. Eventually, feeling only revulsion where once the joy of battle set his spirits soaring, he left Geronimo to follow his own path.

Stopping by a border town called Vernon Wells to buy some ammunition a few days later, he got into a fight with a couple of plug-uglies who made it all too obvious what they thought of 'red-niggers'. He knocked one of them unconscious. The other managed to crack a plank of wood across his skull before the Apache ventilated him with the ten inch blade of his much-loved hunter's Bowie knife.

Stunned and disorientated, he was taken into custody, beaten repeatedly, tried by a jury of bigots and sentenced to hang. The circuit judge, fearing an outbreak of lynch-fever, sent him to Yuma Pen to await the date of his execution. He'd been sweating it out in the prison hot-box when he got word that he had six days left in this life.

But now he was free again. And the knife in his grasp made him feel whole.

Longblade stared off into the far blue distance. It would be easy to disappear into the desert, to find his people up in the Sierra Madres and settle among them again.

Easy, yes.

But the prospect of battle alongside Dark and Chance and the others held more excitement.

Longblade took his dark eyes away from the distant mountains and studied the ground, searching for animal tracks. Game out in this dry land would be scarce, which was why the sergeant, O'Connor, had suggested he hunt jackrabbits. But hefting the knife in his hand, Longblade smiled as he decided to go one better and take back to camp a tender young antelope.

There was only one thing Abel Frost hated worse than being proved wrong, and that was someone else being proved right.

But as he finished off his helpings of doe meat, he consoled himself with the way his six soldiers of misfortune had come together as a team when Longblade returned to camp with a rare smile lighting his usually mournful face and a heavy, blood-stained deer across one broad shoulder.

Indeed, as the animal was butchered and cooked, there was an easier, more relaxed atmosphere down in the dry wash, but instead of enjoying the moment, as O'Connor did, Frost felt his gut clenching in anticipation of the time when things would return to normal.

There was still about seventy miles to the border. By Frost's reckoning they would cross over into Mexico some time tomorrow afternoon and reach Tacalima by dusk. From there it was a simple case of scouting this monastery the Black

Wolf was holed up in, formulating a plan of action, issuing weapons to the men and seeing the whole business through to the bloody end.

Simple, yeah.

Like hell.

Some time later, after tightening up cinches and remounting, they continued on across the land, still keeping to the same invisible southwesterly line. Mile followed mile; five became ten became fifteen. Finally, as the sun began to sink westward, Frost called a halt and they made camp in a sheltered bowl of land that offered reasonable forage for the horses.

'How far d'you figure we are from Spearman?' O'Connor asked as he started to erect a rough but serviceable rope corral.

Frost shrugged. ' 'Bout five miles,' he replied quietly. He'd deliberately called a halt here rather than risk the men going crazy in such a wide open copper town.

'Think I'll ride in now an' pick up those couple items we talked about last night,' said O'Connor.

'Need any comp'ny, sarge?' asked Boone, who had been standing nearby, unsaddling his dun.

Before T T could reply, Dark swaggered over. 'What's that? You say somethin' about a *town*, O'Connor?'

Frost sighed. 'Forget it. Nobody's going anywhere except T T.'

'Now just hold up there, marshal,' the albino replied easily. 'You mean we're only five miles from bright lights an' good whiskey?'

'And soft beds,' said Forrest, coming over.

'Yeah, and softer women,' McCord added with a grin.

'Forget it,' Frost said again.

'I ain't forgettin' it. Are you, boys?'

Forrest, McCord and Chance shook their heads. Boone didn't seem to care one way or the other. Longblade, who had come up to stand behind Dark, kept his face neutral.

'Now you listen up, marshal,' said the albino, ' 'cause I'm only sayin' it the once. We've agreed to take out this Black Wolf jasper ...'

'For a thousand bucks each,' said Frost.

'That ain't the point. We're puttin' our lives on the line for you and that crazy old man, Wilde. The least you can do is let us have a little whoopin' an' hollerin' before we get around to the killin'.'

'Or bein' killed,' muttered Frost menacingly.

'Right,' said Chance, nodding.

Frost looked at each of them. He didn't like it. He didn't like it at all. But what was it T T had told him earlier? To bend a little. He found O'Connor's eyes and searched for guidance, but the NCO only shrugged.

'All right,' Frost decided after one more heartbeat. 'But God help the man who starts any trouble, because Black Wolf or no Black Wolf, if any one of you foul-ups fouls up, I'll make sure you *all* end up back behind bars!'

For more years than it cared to recall, Spearman had been little more than a watering hole for travellers heading north or south to more appealing destinations. Then the surrounding hills began to yield so much copper that all the major mining companies, including Phelps Dodge, the Arizona Copper Company and W A Clark had moved in, set up shop and turned the once-backwater into a virtual metropolis.

Nowadays Spearman catered for all tastes and could hardly relieve the rough-and-ready miners of their wages fast enough. It was a boom town, 'boom' as in explosive. To Abel Frost, it might just as well be a powder keg, with his six prisoners the fuse.

He, O'Connor and the men entered town just as the Presbyterian church on McCandless Street began to toll the hour. It was seven o'clock on a Monday evening and Spearman was just coming to life.

At the corner of Douglas and Cottey, O'Connor reined in his bay and said, 'I'll go pick up those supplies. You be all right, Abel?'

'Yeah, sure,' Frost replied without much enthusiasm. 'We'll go find someplace to eat, then grab a drink ...'

'Or two,' said Dark.

' ... down there,' said Frost, pointing to a saloon half-way down Cottey called *Rita's*.

O'Connor nodded. 'I'll join you there directly.'

Frost and his men found a hash house further along the street and left their horses at the livery next door. Fortunately, the eaterie was still mostly empty, it being the start of the evening, so

there wasn't too much opportunity for the
prisoners to make trouble. Frost, seeing that the
place was run by a skinny little Mexican and his
enormous wife, ordered mincemeat-stuffed tor-
tillas, tostadas, tamales, frijoles, rice and a
sharp-smelling *chilli* sauce, and when it arrived
everyone dug in.

As soon as his plate was clean, Dark pushed it
away and belched his satisfaction. 'Come on you
bastards, eat up, will ya? The marshal's buyin'
drinks over to *Rita's* when you've finished!'

Frost closed his eyes and sighed. He pushed his
own plate away even though he had hardly
touched his meal.

'You finished with that, marshal?' growled
Forrest. Without waiting for a reply he reached
over, took the plate and set about demolishing
Frost's leavings.

Ten minutes later the tall lawman paid the
bill and all seven men left the restaurant. By
now the sky was hooded and homely yellow lights
twinkled up and down the street. Under any other
circumstances Frost would have enjoyed civili-
sation after such a long absence. Right now he
just wanted to get his six potential time-bombs
back on the trail and out of temptation's way.

They crossed the still bustling street and
headed for *Rita's*. Some of the day's furnace heat
had died now and a warm but refreshing breeze
was blowing at their backs. Inside the saloon
Frost scanned the crowd for any sign of O'Connor,
but the Irishman was nowhere to be seen. He led

the men to a vacant table, caught the attention of one idling bartender and ordered seven beers.

'Ah hell, marshal, I thought we might have a little whiskey,' said Dark.

'Who needs whiskey?' remarked Chance, eyeing a nearby percentage girl. 'You wanna advance me some of my thousand bucks, marshal? I sure could use me some funnin' after spendin' two nights in handcuffs!'

Just then the beer arrived, but only six schooners of it.

'You're one short,' Frost told the bartender.

'No I ain't,' replied the man. He was small and thirty-five, with black hair and a dark, weasel's face. He looked dapper in his white shirt, black string tie and crisp white apron as he indicated Longblade. 'We don't serve injuns.'

The Apache's thin mouth turned down at the corners and he made to rise, but Boone, seated beside him, clapped one big black hand on his arm. Longblade froze.

'You'll serve *this* injun,' the negro said quietly.

The bartender looked at him as life went on laughing and gaming and drinking around him. Frost wondered if he should take a hand or watch how his men handled themselves. He decided to sit tight.

'It's nothing personal,' the bartender replied uneasily. 'It's just the rules.'

'Sure, we know about rules,' said Dark, smiling nastily. 'We know how to make 'em and how to break 'em. You savvy?'

The bartender started to flush. 'Look, you can always try drinkin' someplace else ...'

'Yeah, but we've settled *here*, butt-crust,' said Forrest. 'Now, you're one beer light, like the marshal here says. Go get it.'

The bartender sighed. 'Ah hell, okay. But ...'

'Just get it.'

Frost picked up his own glass and sampled the brew to hide the sudden and unexpected surge of pleasure that the confrontation had brought on. All of these men were individuals, as O'Connor had said. But in the face of a common enemy – albeit just a prissy little bartender – they had fused together as a team. The marshal could hardly believe it – but years of experience had taught him not to count chickens.

As they nursed their beers, waiting for O'Connor to arrive, Frost filled them in on what little he knew about the outlaw they were being sent after. The men showed more interest in the whores drumming up trade around them. When he could sense their restlessness growing to danger level, he decided to call it a day. Christ alone knew where O'Connor was. He would just have to meet up with them back at their original campsite.

'All right boys, party's over. Let's be making tracks.'

'Aw come on, marsh ...'

'You heard what I said.'

Surprisingly, Dark was first on his feet. 'Hold up, marshal. I gotta go to the john afore I go anyplace else.'

Frost gave a mental curse. 'Can't it wait until we're out of town?'

'Could you wait after tostadas, tamales and frijoles?' the albino asked. He indicated the side door that led out to the backyard and the privvies located there. 'It won't take long, I can promise you that!'

Frost thought fast. He couldn't send one prisoner to guard another; the chances were that they'd both escape. Likewise, if he went with Dark, the other men would be left unguarded. For a moment he considered trooping all six of them out back together until he remembered what O'Connor had said about self-respect and how a man could respond to it. Apart from which, if Dark tried to escape now, he'd be running out on a thousand dollars.

The albino rubbed at his stomach, his expression pained.

'Make it quick then,' Frost muttered.

Dark beamed. 'As quick as I can.'

'And remember; I'm trusting you, Dark. We all are.'

The albino weaved through the throng and disappeared out back.

Three treacle-slow minutes later O'Connor came through the batwings. By this time the level of noise had risen and the air was turning blue with cigarette smoke. The NCO looked around, saw Frost and the others seated around the table and edged his way towards them.

'Oooh boy! You wouldn't believe how hard it is to get ...'

Only when Frost stood up did the Irishman notice his grim expression. 'Stay with the men, T T!'

Without stopping to explain more, Frost pushed through the crowd to disappear out the side door.

The back yard was a twenty-foot cobbled square surrounded by a six foot high plank wall. Moonlight spilled across the two wooden privvies in the far left corner and the piles of junk left everywhere else. Frost heard the sounds of rats above the muted merriment behind him. He crossed the yard, checked both privvies.

Empty.

His curse was direct and colourful, and cut short by a sudden blast of gunfire.

He ran for the nearest wall, leapt up and over into the alleyway beyond, his mind racing. The gunfire had come from the south, not too far south, either. Chances were it had nothing to do with Dark, but then again ...

Frost burst out of the alleymouth into Douglas Street, fearing the worst. The crowd of towns-people up around the porch of a general store seventy-five yards away did nothing to improve his mood. Hurriedly he followed a number of locals up the street towards the scene of the commotion.

The store was called *Grady's*. There was a dead man lying just in front of the doorway. Grady stood over him looking slightly lost. Six feet from the body, a pair of burly town constables held Nathan Dark with his arms shoved halfway up his back while a pot-bellied town marshal held an impromptu inquest. The entire scene was lit by a swaying storm lantern.

Frost pushed through the crowd and when the town marshal turned to ask just what in hell he was playing at, Frost flipped open the wallet containing his badge.

'Abel Frost, Deputy United States Marshal,' he said with authority. His angry grey eyes burned into the albino although his question was aimed at the other lawman. 'What's going on here?'

The town marshal spat on the boardwalk. 'By cracky, you gov'mint fellers sure don't waste any time, do you?' he asked laconically. He was in his late fifties and his voice had the same grating, unfriendly quality as jagged glass. 'I'm Sid Berner, town law. And as to what's been goin' on here, well, it's a clear-cut case of attempted horse-theft and murder.'

'Oh?'

Berner nodded. 'The deceased, Ben Cooke, was inside with Grady, buyin' some supplies, when this apparition here – ' he indicated Dark, who stiffened indignantly, ' – came racin' along the boardwalk like a bat out'n hell. Ben turns to see what all the noise is about and spies yonder al-bi-no tryin' to make off with his hoss.' Berner's nicotine-stained index finger pointed toward a sleepy-looking pinto mare tied to the hitch rack. 'Ben comes out –'

'Yeah, wavin' a goddamn six-shooter,' Dark spat.

'There's a scuffle,' Berner went on, 'and the next thing we know, ol' Ben's ezzactly as you see him now and this here feller bein' *re*-strained by my men is standin' over him with the gun in his fist.'

Frost let his breath out slowly. He felt angry and irritated, more at his own curious compulsion to try and help Dark than anything else. 'I don't want you to think I'm stepping on your toes, marshal,' he said politely. 'I mean, I know this is your bailiwick and all. But do you mind if I get the, uh, albino's side of it?'

'Go ahead.'

Frost returned his gaze to Dark. 'Well? Let's hear it.'

Dark looked hurt. 'These guys got it all wrong. I'm comin' up the street, right? I see this horse lookin' all tired an' beat up. I reach out to give it a stroke on account of me havin' this thing about horseflesh. Next thing I know, this dead guy's comin' at me with his iron.'

'You mean you shot him by accident?' asked Berner.

'Sure,' Dark replied, deadpan, 'Well, more like self-defence.'

Frost shook his head. Even he couldn't help a man with a story as cock-eyed as that. No – Dark had betrayed Frost's trust, made a run for it, tried to steal a horse and got caught in the act. The lawman shook his head again. He told himself that Dark deserved everything he had coming.

'Satisfied, marshal?' Berner asked suddenly.

Frost looked straight into the albino's scarecrow face. 'Yeah,' he replied softly, his jaw muscles working.

'Okay, boys. Take him away.'

As the two deputies started to drag him off to the lock-ups, Dark threw one last look over his shoulder. 'Hey, Frost! Tell 'em it's the truth! Tell 'em how much I love horses! *Frost!*'

But Frost only turned away and pushed back through the hostile crowd.

Seven

McCord's usually cheerful face was dark with anger. 'Sonofabitch,' he muttered.

The rest of the men, still seated around the table in the saloon, shared his fury, for Frost had just returned to tell them about Dark's ill-fated escape attempt and the murder of what he had since discovered to be a very popular figure around the town.

'Son-of-a-*bitch*,' McCord said again.

Frost let his eyes rake over them, then lifted his empty schooner to get the bartender's attention. When he had it he mouthed his order, and a little while later seven more beers arrived.

They drank, then fell silent again, until Boone finally asked, 'So what happens now?'

Frost shrugged. His frustration was obvious. 'Like the town law said, it's a clear-cut case of attempted horse theft and murder. Dark'll stand trial, and if this guy Ben Cooke had as many friends hereabouts as I hear tell, he'll hang.'

'I meant about *us*,' said Boone quietly.

Frost lowered his eyes to his beer, not answering.

'The deal off, marshal?' asked McCord.

'What he means is, you sendin' us back to Yuma on account of Dark?' Chance demanded bluntly.

Frost lifted his mug, took a long swallow to give himself some time to think. He was not a man who gave threats lightly, but now that it came to it, he was strangely reluctant to make good on his promise to send these men back to the Pen. Confused by his own indecision, he took another pull at the beer before looking up again.

'I ...'

But before he could say more, a big man with a scarred face and bouncer written all over him, came over and bent so that he could speak straight into the marshal's right ear.

'I'd get out of here fast if I was you, mister. Lot of Ben Cooke's buddies use this place. Don't reckon they take kindly to drinkin' 'longside friends of his killer.'

Frost narrowed his eyes and scanned the crowd behind his men for the first time. Suddenly he became aware of the hostile looks he and the Wilde boys were getting from a number of hard-faced miner-types, and realised that the level of noise had dropped to a dangerous, growling babble. He looked up at the bouncer and fingered his moustache.

'Obliged,' he said shortly.

As the bouncer sauntered away, Frost got to his feet and Forrest asked what was going on.

'We're leaving,' Frost replied quietly. He led the men towards the batwings and then out into the night with O'Connor bringing up the rear.

The night-blanketed street was strangely quiet now, although further south, in Spearman's red-light district, tinkling pianos, breaking glass and high-pitched feminine laughter confirmed that hell was still splitting its corsets somewhere. Frost started along Cottey Street, heading for the livery where they'd left their horses and the men followed without complaint.

They were halfway down the street when they heard it.

'Come on then! Let's hang the bastard!'

Frost and the Wilde boys spun back to face the saloon just as the batwings crashed open and a torrent of thirty-odd angry, liquored-up miners flooded out into the lamp-lit street. The tall lawman watched as the crowd began to surge north, away from them, then turn left into Douglas Street, heading for Marshal Berner's office.

Frost, O'Connor, Boone and the others stood in the centre of the street, watching the blood-hungry lynch mob move off. The skin on each man's face was tight and cold.

'Jesus God, marshal. We just gon' stand by and watch 'em string Dark up?' asked Boone.

'No,' Frost replied grimly. 'We're gonna get the hell out of here before they try to string *us* up, too.'

He turned away and started back in the direction of the livery stable.

Chance cocked his head. 'Hey, marshal. I thought it was your job to stop other folks from breakin' the law.'

Frost nodded. 'It is. But I don't reckon a mob like that'd pay much attention to me.'

Or Marshal Berner, come to that, he added silently.

Slowly, almost reluctantly, the men began following him again.

'Poor ole Dark,' said Boone.

'Yeah. I reckon that crazy bastard was born to hang,' McCord agreed, his irritation of a few minutes before now forgotten.

Chance was the one who finally came out and said what they were all thinking. 'I reckon we oughtta go back and help him.'

Frost continued walking. 'Why? You don't owe *him* anything, Chance. He ran out on all of us.'

'Yeah, but a *lynch*-mob ...'

They made it into the livery, where a single lamp, trimmed low, cast a feeble, mustard-coloured glow over the interior. Frost strode directly across the hay-strewn floor to the stall which contained his appaloosa, ignoring his own irrational urge to go back and help a man he didn't even like, then realised that O'Connor and the five convicts were still crowded in the doorway.

'Come on, let's get *out* of here,' he barked.

The men stayed where they were.

Frost fingered his moustache. 'I said ...'

'Abel,' O'Connor interrupted calmly. 'They want to go back an' help their friend.'

Frost glared at them with mockery in his eyes. 'Oh yeah? And what do you think *you* can do against thirty or forty drunken miners?'

Longblade glanced at his fellow prisoners, then back to the lawman. 'Just give us a chance and you'll find out,' he replied softly.

Nathan Dark sat on the edge of the bunk in his tiny, unswept cell and cursed his luck. If the cards had fallen differently, he'd have been out of this town by now and heading north or west for healthier climes. It wasn't his fault that he'd chosen the wrong horse to steal, or that the owner of said animal was eagle-eyed and trigger-happy.

Again he swore bitterly, although this time his anger was directed at Abel Frost. He might have known that big bastard wouldn't rush to help him. That guy had had it in for him right from the start. But he promised himself that he'd get even. Somehow. He glared murderously through the thick iron bars at Marshal Berner and his two bully-boy town constables, but they only ignored him.

He lay back on the bunk, forcing himself to calm down and figure a way out of his predicament. If he could just get his hands on a gun ... but hell, that was impossible. There had to be another way.

It was at that moment that he and the three peace-keepers became aware of a distant babble floating through the warm evening air. Voices. Raised. Angry. Coming closer.

Dark had spent enough years falling in and out of trouble to know what it meant. As panic stabbed him in the gut he came up off the bunk and clutched the bars of the cell. 'Hey, what's goin' on out there?'

Marshal Berner got up from behind his desk and joined his deputies at the thick wooden door. The three of them stood looking out into the night while Dark strangled the bars of his cell impatiently.

'Uh-oh,' said Berner after a moment. 'I sure as hell don't like the look of this.'

'The look'a what?' demanded Dark.

But by now the menacing sounds of male voices and the stomping of many heavy boots had grown to such a volume that Dark didn't really need to be told.

The two deputies looked pale in the spill of bright lantern-light. 'What we gonna do, marshal?' asked the biggest.

Town Marshal Sid Berner looked at the approaching band of florid-faced mine-workers and wiped a hand across his sweaty top lip. There were between forty and fifty of them. Some carried clubs, others old and badly-kept long guns. A few more carried flaming torches that scattered a restless red hell-glow over them. The man in the lead, a good friend of the late Ben Cooke whose name was Harry Page, held a crudely-fashioned noose.

The mob came to a halt in front of the law office. All along the street, people had come to doors and windows to see what must inevitably happen next.

' 'Evenin' Sid,' Harry Page said with a curt nod. 'You know why we're here, so I won't waste time explainin'. I'll just say that we can do it the hard way or we can do it th' easy way. 'S'entirely up to you.'

Marshal Berner sucked in his gut and took a reluctant step forward. Although he had had no previous experience at handling vigilantes, he knew he must adopt a serious and authoritarian stance. A ripple went through the sea of flushed, angry and expectant faces spread before him.

'That feller in the cell back there's a prisoner of these United States,' he said importantly. 'He'll be tried fair'n'square by a duly-appointed judge an' jury. Hellfire, Harry, I 'preciate that Ben Cooke was a friend o' yourn, but this is 1880! Lynch mobs are a thing of the past. And they sure ain't gonna be tolerated in *this* town by *this* law officer!'

'Oh yeah?' sneered a fat-faced man beside Page. He brought up an ugly sawed-off shotgun and thumbed back both hammers. The man was so close to him that Berner thought he might fall right into one of the barrels.

'All right!' he yelped, deciding that Dark wasn't worth dying for. 'Bring that bastard out here, Artie! These good citizens want a hangin', and that's what they're gonna get!'

A cheer went up as one of the deputies went back into the jail to get Dark. The albino could hardly share their enthusiasm. In fact, he was already finding it difficult to breathe.

The deputy, Artie, produced a ring of keys, selected one and unlocked the cell door. Dark stepped back, trying mightily to stop his red eyes from dropping to the big constable's sidearm and telegraphing his by-now desperate intention.

'I sure am sorry about this,' the deputy said apologetically. He seemed to mean it, too. 'But you gotta understand the marshal's p'sition. I mean, we gotta *live* with those people out there.'

'Yeah, yeah,' Dark mumbled irritably.

Artie swung the cell door inwards, then stepped back a pace. 'Out you come,' he said a little more cheerfully.

Dark moved forward on legs like jelly. He'd seen quite a few neck-stretchings in his time and none of them had been pretty. Black and bloated faces with staring-fit-to-pop eyes, snapped necks a foot or more in length, the awful stench of burst bowels ... He forced the horrors to the back of his mind and stepped out of the cell. Artie was about three feet away. Dark tensed his arms and legs, preparing to pounce.

Then the other deputy appeared in the doorway.

Damn.

There was a panicky edge to the man's voice. 'C'mon, hurry it up, Artie! These guys're gettin' impatient out here!'

Dark's shoulders slumped. For one split-second he was tempted to make a grab for Artie's sidearm just to force the other deputy to shoot him, figuring it was better to die from lead than hemp. But then Artie clapped one big paw on his shoulder and shoved him across the office and out onto the porch.

As soon as he appeared, another cheer went up

from the crowd, but it wasn't the 'hip-hip-hooray' kind. These bastards wanted blood. It just so happened they wanted *his* blood. He glared at the sharp-etched, drunken faces glaring back at him and spat.

'All right. Come an' get me!'

Harry Page stepped forward with the hangrope twisted between his knuckly fists and got one foot up on the boardwalk before a gunshot cracked through the uproar.

Silence fell like a cloudburst. And into the silence came the sound of footsteps. Slow, deliberate, unstoppable.

'What in ...'

Abel Frost appeared from out of the shadows further down the boardwalk, holding a Winchester repeater. A spectral wisp of smoke was still snaking from the barrel.

Not a word was spoken until the grey-eyed lawman joined Dark, Berner and his two deputies in front of the jail.

'Boy, am I glad to ...'

Frost spoke without taking his eyes off the lynch-mob. 'Shut it, Dark.'

Dark nodded eagerly. 'Sure, sure.'

Frost nodded to Harry Page, but his unsettling eyes kept moving over the hard-looking men behind him. 'If I didn't know better,' he said dryly, 'I'd say you fellers was up to no good.'

Page pulled a face. 'Ah, get outta the way! We're dispensin' justice here! In case you didn't know it, this sonuver you're stickin' up for just kilt a man!'

'Oh, he knows all right, Harry!' cried a hot-head further back in the crowd. 'I seen him drinkin' wi' thet murderer no more'n a half-hour back!'

Harry Page looked at Frost with new interest, nodding slowly. 'All *right*. You're stickin' up for your friend. I c'n 'preciate that. But it so happens that Ben Cooke was a friend o' *mine*, so step aside, neighbour, unless you want to make this a double hangin'!'

The crowd's roar of encouragement hit Frost like a knuckle-duster, but still he faced the lynch-mob head-on, and after a while they simmered down some to hear what he had to say next.

What he said was simple and direct. 'I've got five men set up all around you fellers, and there's not a-one of them afraid to pull a trigger.'

'Huh? What's that s'posed t'mean?' Page asked warily.

'Just that the first man here who tries to start this necktie party rolling gets a navel where he doesn't need one,' Frost replied, pinning all his attention on the other man. 'Think about it, *neighbour*. Do you really want to turn a hanging into a bloodbath?'

Harry Page allowed his eyes to drop from Frost's thin face. For a long moment he was silent, as were they all. Page didn't want any arguments with Judge Colt, just like any man with half a lick of sense, but feeling the weight of the men behind him, he knew he could not back down without some show of defiance.

'How do I know you ain't bluffin'?' he snarled.

Frost didn't reply, he didn't need to. The sound of shells being pumped into five long guns coming from the shadows surrounding the lynch-mob painted a vivid enough picture.

Page hissed something unintelligible.

A sudden clatter of horses' hooves fragmented the otherwise silent night. Some of the men in the crowd chanced a slow look behind them and saw T T O'Connor and five of the Wilde boys walking their horses slowly down the street towards them, fanned out and with Winchesters aimed steady. The NCO held the reins to Frost's appaloosa and Dark's pinto. They halted about ten feet from the frozen miners.

'Move,' Frost hissed to Dark.

He and the albino did just that, while the lynch-mob was still off-balance. They skirted the crowd, relying on their comrades to cover them if Page or his buddies tried to get clever, then threw themselves up into their saddles.

'I'll have your guts for this!' Page yelled angrily. 'All of you!'

By way of reply, Frost touched the brim of his hat and smiled. Then he and his men wheeled their horses around in a cloud of dust and cut a fast trail out of town.

Frost and the Wilde boys continued southwest with Dark keeping one red eye on their backtrail and the lawman keeping both his grey eyes on his now-armed prisoners.

Despite his undoubted popularity, however, it appeared that friends of the late Ben Cooke were not as prepared to take the law into their own hands in the sobering light of day as they had been that night. There was no pursuit.

When the men crossed into Mexico some-sixty miles later, they looked exactly like the bristly bunch of no-goods that they were, but they encountered no further trouble. The barren strip of land that separated the north from the south was not greatly populated, and they moved over it unhindered.

Neither did the character of the land change greatly. Scattered rocks and boulders added the colour of slate to the otherwise deadening tan and yellow of the terrain. Mesquite trees grew low and spindly. Cholla and opuntia studded the region.

At the end of their fourth day on the trail, Frost called a halt at the last reasonable body of grass before entering the fearsome *Gran Desierto*. Squinting out across the harsh, bare land that stretched beyond the verdant fringe, he estimated that Tacalima lay about five miles further south.

Both the marshal and his men had no illusions about what they were being sent to do. The governments of both countries wanted that vipers' nest cleaned out, and they'd made it plain that they weren't bothered how Frost got the job done. But the tall lawman needed some idea of his target before he could decide how best to handle it.

As the men unsaddled their horses, rubbed

them down and then set about making a smoke-less fire over which to warm coffee and cook bacon, Frost scanned the bleak horizon. It was little more than a series of gentle, sandy folds.

The attack would have to be made under cover of night, he decided. But in order to plan the next step of the campaign, he needed more information about the monastery; position, layout, the number of men working for the Wolf ...

He decided to send Chance and McCord out to have a look around. Crossing to the fire just as the sky began to streak with the approaching night, he told them what he wanted them to find out. Their complaints came more from habit than anything else, but once they got the bitching out of the way, both men got to their feet and slung canteens across their shoulders. Chance decided that to get into and out of Tacalima unannounced, they would travel light, and a-foot.

'Expect us back around two or three in the mornin',' he growled.

'Aw ... Does that mean I don't get to curl up in my blankets tonight, Chance?' McCord whined.

'Yeah. Tough, ain't it? Now come on, let's get movin'.'

Frost watched the two men nod farewells to the others, then start up one grass-patched slope and disappear behind the ridge it formed. Almost against his will he confessed to a warm feeling of comradeship with them. Then he took a cup of coffee from O'Connor, who gave him a knowing look, and found a seat some way away from the others in which to brood undisturbed.

All right, so he felt a bond with them. But did they feel any such loyalty to *him*? For all he knew, he might never see Chance and McCord ever again. Now that they were in Mexico, it would be easy for them to disappear. Lord knew, it was a big enough country; Frost would have to be damned lucky to ever find them again. Why, even now they might be plotting to join up with the Black Wolf instead of spy on him, to sell the lawman and the other Wilde boys out.

Suddenly he began to grow restless, and the low spirits he'd suffered that first day out on the trail threatened to come back and swamp him. But as full dark descended on the men and their meagre campfire, Frost decided he had nothing to gain from worrying about it. Like it or not, he had no choice in the matter but to trust them.

It took Chance and McCord just over two hours to reach Tacalima. By then the last of the day's heat had been sucked into the ground and a sharp desert chill had started to gnaw at their bones.

The two convicts hunkered down in a scattering of brush about a hundred yards outside town, watching for signs of life, but the jumble of ill-matched adobe dwellings was silent and wrapped in darkness even though it was only a little after 10 pm.

McCord quickly ran his bleached blue eyes over the sleeping structures. Both men had agreed that there was little point in wasting time scouting the town. Their prime target was the monastery on the hill, so that was where they would concentrate their attention.

'Fit?' Chance asked in a whisper.

McCord took his eyes off the town and nodded.

The two Wilde boys moved on, swinging a wide loop around Tacalima and heading west. Neither man made much noise crossing the wrinkled desert floor. Their movements were swift, silent and shadow-like beneath the uncertain starlight. But for the water sloshing in their canteens, they might have been phantoms.

Somewhere a dog howled, but that was the only sound. Then the town was behind them and they felt the ground begin to slope upwards beneath their boots. They went into a crouch at the foot of the sage-scented hill.

Even nightfall could not disguise the brooding menace that spilled from the monastery above.

As a stronghold, it was impressive. McCord estimated it to be about a hundred and fifty feet square, and its twenty-foot high walls looked to be thick and secure. But before he could move in closer, Chance touched him on the arm and pointed. McCord followed his aim and saw a man in the watch-tower above the wooden gates. He nodded; from here on, they would walk on eggs.

Slowly they circled the monastery, studying it from the base of the hill. The only way in or out was the two thick gates at the front, but there was a section of the otherwise-blank west wall that had crumbled and might offer another means of entrance.

That established, they left their canteens in among some sagebrush and began to move cautiously up the hill. Making it to the base of the ruined wall, they edged along to the spot where part of it had fallen in. Chance made a stirrup of his hands and McCord set one boot into it, allowing the other man to boost him up.

He grabbed the top of the wall; dust and little chunks of adobe shifted beneath his fingers. Finally he got a firm hold and swung one leg over the wall, peering back into Chance's up-turned face to give a thumbs-up.

'Make it quick!' Chance whispered urgently.

McCord nodded, then slipped down the rubble on the other side of the wall.

He was in an alleyway between two buildings, a stable and some kind of bunkhouse. Someone was playing a banjo inside the building on his left. Someone else was laughing. A woman. He edged into the mouth of the alley and scanned the courtyard, with its ornate fountain, fixing buildings and distances in his mind.

The man up in the watch-tower, who was peering out into the darkness, appeared to be the only one on guard, which suited McCord fine. He slipped out into the courtyard and eased along the bunkhouse wall until he reached one shuttered window. The aimless plucking of the banjo sounded louder now, as did the woman's tinkling laughter and the idle card-game chatter of a group of men inside. As McCord bent to peer through a gap in the shutter, he heard a door open further along the wall and quickly dodged back into the shadowed alleyway.

The man who came out into the courtyard was short and thin and dressed in a dusty black suit. McCord narrowed his eyes in recognition almost immediately. Frost had told them about this character. He'd even shown them a dodger featuring the man's likeness.

It was Crazy Bob Jarvis.

Beyond the outlaw, in the shadows around the opposite wall, McCord detected more movement and decided that the place was getting too busy for the unhurried look-around he'd hoped for.

He turned and headed back towards the mountain of rubble beneath the crumbling wall when suddenly he heard a gun coming to full cock and a harsh voice yell,

'Hold it right there!'

Eight

Ten seconds passed before McCord realised that the voice had not been aimed at him. Then, feeling relieved and curious, he turned and cat-footed back to the alleymouth just as the man in the watch-tower peered down into the courtyard and asked what was going on.

Jarvis had the drop on the man McCord had seen in the shadows opposite just a few seconds earlier. What he had taken to be one of the Black Wolf's men was obviously another intruder.

Five men spilled out of the bunkhouse with guns drawn, and at the sight of them McCord drew back, his right hand dropping to his own Peacemaker. Meanwhile, Jarvis had grabbed hold of the intruder's arm and shoved him roughly towards the centre of the courtyard, where the light from the now-open door would illuminate him.

More men began to appear from other low-roofed buildings, eleven, twelve ... fourteen in all, including the massive slab-shouldered black man with the chipped teeth and bandolier who McCord knew must be Joshua Thorne, the Black Wolf.

Jarvis dug his fingers into the intruder's hair and pulled his head back hard, but the man did not cry out although it was obvious from his expression that he was in considerable pain. McCord could see that he was in his early twenties, with a prematurely aged but otherwise open and honest set of features. He was dressed in the uniform of the United States Army, and apparently he was a lieutenant.

Jarvis and the Wolf were talking rapidly to one another now, and although McCord couldn't make out what was being said, it was obvious that the discovery of a soldier in their stronghold had spooked them.

McCord tried to make sense of what was happening, but knew he couldn't afford to stick around much longer. If anybody spotted him now, they'd almost certainly shoot first and ask questions later. Besides which, he now had a good idea of numbers and layout that Frost could begin to work from.

He turned and made his way back towards the ruined wall just as the Black Wolf back-handed the lieutenant, softening him up for the interrogation to come.

Lieutenant Warren Baxter, from Roanoke, Virginia, knew that his men thought he'd gone crazy the minute he picked up his Springfield and Colt and went in search of his horse.

But as he climbed into the saddle of his

still-skittish bay and began to follow the deep wheel-ruts his payroll wagon had made in the sandy soil, he realised that he did not care. He had only one thought in mind as he began to track the outlaws; revenge.

Baxter came from a long line of high-ranking military men. It was a proud boast among his family that there had been a Baxter man at every major skirmish his country had ever seen, and not one of them had ever done less than his sacred duty on the battlefield.

Thus, it galled the young lieutenant to recall the disgraceful way he had acted under fire when his detachment had been ambushed at Firewater Creek. Trembling, unable to help or organise his men.

Warren Baxter knew he would never be able to live with himself unless he did something to redress the balance. He could not let his family down any more than he could wipe away the memory of his poor, murdered men. So he followed the tracks of the payroll wagon mile after mile, not so much a man any more as an automaton, and his thoughts centred only on making things right again and easing his conscience.

He was not aware of the passage of time, nor of hunger, thirst or fatigue. All he knew was the wheel-ruts and the horse-tracks stretching on into the distance. And revenge.

At last he reached Tacalima, and rightly assumed the monastery on the hill to be the outlaws' hideout. He had watched the place as darkness gathered, then made his way up to the stronghold. He had not given much thought to what he would do to these men, nor of how slim his chances were once among them. All he craved now was the opportunity to strike back. ◑

Ironically, he had gained entrance to the monastery by the same route as McCord, and only a scant fifteen minutes earlier, by which time the soldier in him began to take over and he found himself looking upon his task not so much as a mission of vengeance as a short, sharp military campaign to be executed with resolve and cunning.

Until he'd been spotted.

And now, as the Black Wolf and Jarvis and Will Slade and the other hard-faced men gathered menacingly around him, it looked like he would die a slow and ignominious death before he could even the balance.

Warren Baxter would let his family, his men and saddest of all, himself down one final, bitter time.

It was a little after two in the morning when Chance and McCord made it back to camp. Their arrival roused all but Frost, who'd been keeping watch for them. As O'Connor used a stick to jab the fire back to life, McCord recounted what had happened to a circle of grim, expectant faces.

At the end of it, Boone said, 'Well, that just about puts a lid on it, huh, marshal? I mean, now this sojer-boy's turned up, that Black Wolf's gonna be on his guard, ain't he?'

'Yeah,' Dark cut in before the lawman could reply. 'We ain't gonna get nowhere near that place now, Frost.'

Frost said nothing, although he had to agree that the appearance of this mysterious Army officer certainly was going to make a difficult job worse. Who was he anyway? And what business did he have nosing around the Black Wolf's hideout? Frost tried to figure a connection but couldn't.

'If you got any sense, marshal, you'll call the whole thing off,' said Dark. 'Or leastways put it back a while until those owlhoots start gettin' careless again.'

Again Frost made no comment. Putting the job back would only give his men more of an opportunity to run out on him, and calling it off might make Washington cancel Judge Wilde's project altogether – which would mean sending the Wilde boys back to the Pen.

'Better face up to it, boys,' he said at length. 'We're going through with it, whether you like it or not.'

'Huh?' said O'Connor, who, in light of what McCord had told them, clearly thought it was better to wait.

'You heard what I said,' Frost gritted. 'We're not calling it off and we're not putting it back. Just the opposite, in fact. We're going to hit the Black Wolf at first light.' He took out his Ingersoll and checked the time. 'That's about three hours from now.'

He'd expected resistance. They wouldn't have been the Wilde boys if they hadn't put up a fight. But in the end, even they had to admit the wisdom of his decision.

His reasoning was simple; if they were to stand any chance at all, they had to strike quickly, while the outlaws were still off-balance. They had to catch them while they were still spooked, before they could organise themselves and prepare for any coming conflict.

Frost outlined his plan fast, and McCord helped fill in the gaps as he went along. The attack was to be two-pronged. It would rely on speed and surprise and the supplies O'Connor had bought in Spearman.

'When we get to it, it'll be you or them,' the lawman concluded. 'Remember that. But at the same time, keep an eye open for those whores McCord says they've got in there. They're not part of the gang, got it?'

'Yeah, but they ain't exactly *innocent* either, are they?' Dark said, rolling his eyes.

Frost checked the time again. 'All right. You know what you've got to do. Just make sure that when the time comes, you *do* it. Now, get your gear together. We're moving out. Oh, and one last thing.'

The men froze in the act of gathering blankets and buckling gunbelts.

'I'll kill any man here who tries to get smart and switch sides when we get in there. Like I said, it'll be *us* against *them*.'

No-one spoke.

'All right,' the marshal said again, fingering his moustache ominously. 'Let's do it.'

Few men think of death as a new day comes to life. Their minds are still fogged by dreams, their thoughts – when they do coalesce – usually focused on that first cup of coffee or cigarette that will get them started.

At least that's what Abel Frost hoped as he checked the time once again.

5:15 am.

He let his breath out in a long, calming stream, then looked at the men watching him. Boone, Chance and Forrest were all huddled at the base of the monastery's ruined west wall, all of them wearing sidearms and carrying their brand-new Winchesters strapped across their backs. They looked anxious, keyed-up, but ready.

Frost turned his eyes skyward. Dawn creeps up on a man, he thought. Few are ever aware of that first promise of gold along the eastern horizon. Many are too bleary-eyed to notice the splash of pink that bounces off the bellies of the scudding clouds. The lightening of the sky is a gradual thing, only reaching its final clear blue destination after a slow journey through a thousand shades of black and purple and grey.

Dawn is a time to wake slowly and prepare

yourself for the coming day. It is quiet, relaxing, peaceful.

It is also a good time to kill.

He checked the time again. 5:20. The others should be in position by now.

They'd made good time after quitting their campsite three hours before. They'd swung a wide loop around Tacalima, hobbled their horses in a grama-stitched gully about half a mile away and approached the Black Wolf's stronghold from the blank west wall.

Reaching the base of the hill while night still claimed the sky, they went over the plan one more time in sharp, urgent whispers. Then O'Connor, Dark, McCord and Longblade split away from the others, heading for the two oak gates at the front of the monastery, while Frost led the rest up to the crumbling west wall.

There was no backing out now. They were committed. The attack was about to begin.

The bow in Sam Longblade's hard left fist meant almost as much to him as the Bowie blade O'Connor had returned to him a few days earlier. It was an impressive weapon made from juniper and buffalo sinew, and Longblade preferred it to the rifle O'Connor had issued him for many – mostly practical – reasons.

Now, as they all went down on their bellies and looked up at the worn trail leading to the heavy oak gates, the NCO put one hand on the Apache's shoulder and said, 'Sure you know what to do?'

Longblade's teeth flashed white through the gloom. 'Just watch.'

He moved away before O'Connor could say more, covering the open ground in a half-crouch. And then, so suddenly that McCord could not help but give a low whistle of admiration, the half-breed seemed to disappear right into the earth. O'Connor, Dark and McCord narrowed their eyes, trying to find him, but to no avail.

'Boy, I'm sure glad that Injun's on our side,' Dark muttered.

When he was about seventy feet from the monastery gates, Longblade came up into a kneeling position and slowly reached behind him to draw an arrow from the quiver along his back. It was a lethal-looking thing, fletched with the feathers of a buzzard and tipped with a barbed flint head. Not once did he take his eyes off the man in the watch-tower above the gates as he set the arrow against the taut string.

Slowly he brought the bow up to line. He sighted along the arrow's length with one eye shut, then, only when he was sure he would achieve the kind of swift, silent killing shot that Frost had asked for, did he fire.

The arrow flew straight and true. The guard in the watch-tower never knew what hit him. The arrow went straight through his neck, pinning his scream to the back of his throat. He stumbled a bit, the head of the shaft protruding from the nape of his neck, then caved in.

O'Connor saw the whole thing through his field

glasses. For a second he was silent. Then he got to his feet and together, he, Dark and McCord made it up the hill in the same kind of shambling crouch that the half-breed had used.

'Good work,' the NCO hissed when they reached Longblade. 'No, come on. Let's do what we came for.'

'You sure you know what you're doin' with that stuff?' Dark asked, pointing to the bag slung over O'Connor's left shoulder.

'Dynamite an' blastin' caps?' the Irishman replied with a wicked grin. 'You just wait an' see.'

5:22.

Frost found himself thinking about what Judge Wilde had said the night before they'd started out on this assignment. *The law is like a spider's web. All the little flies get stuck in it, but the big ones crash straight on through. Starting from now, we – you, me and those men over there – we're going to make sure that justice catches up with all those big flies.*

Frost smiled grimly. Well, he thought, they don't come any bigger than the Wolf.

5:24.

He sucked in a chill breath. Here it was at last; the moment of truth. Would his six men turn out to be the foul-ups he had claimed them to be all along, or would they come together as the law-enforcement team Isaac Wilde had said they would when the chips were down?

5:25.

The new day was absolutely silent. Forrest stifled a yawn. Then –

Then hell started popping.

The two explosions that tore the monastery gates off their hinges was just the invitation Frost had been waiting for. Without having to be told, Forrest made a stirrup of his hands and boosted Frost, Boone and Chance up and over the caved-in wall one after the other, then allowed Boone and Chance to haul him up after them.

Meanwhile, the first few outlaws to burst out of their bunkhouse – formerly the monks' cells – were met by a cloud of dust where the gates had been and a withering barrage of rifle fire from O'Connor, Dark, McCord and Longblade.

One man twisted and grabbed his left arm. The outlaw nearest him hauled him back into the relative safety of the building. The rest followed fast, loosing off wild, hasty return fire.

Frost and his men came to a halt in the mouth of the alley between the bunkhouse and the stable. They were breathing hard, but not from exertion. As the lawman scanned the courtyard, he heard the men behind him unlimbering their Winchesters.

Professionals, he thought.

Now that the thunder of the explosions had died away, the marshal became aware of more sounds. A few of the men inside the bunkhouse were yelling to each other above the frenzied screaming of the Black Wolf's imported whores. They were in complete disarray. But although the rattle of their return fire was disjointed, it wouldn't take them long to organise themselves. After all, they were professionals too.

As O'Connor and his men burst through the dust cloud with Winchesters blazing, a few of the owlhoots smashed the bunkhouse windows in order to return fire more effectively. The Wilde boys only just made it to the cover of the fountain before a sudden volley from the bunkhouse peppered the ornate stonework.

Frost jacked a bullet into his own rifle, but from his angle he couldn't do much to set up covering fire for his comrades. He had to find a better position – but to do that he needed some cover of his own.

More gunfire thundered through the new-born day. From the stable next door he heard the nervous whinnyings and stampings of the outlaws' horses.

He turned back to his men. 'Chance – we need a diversion out here, fast.'

'I know it, marshal.'

'Think you can stampede those horses next door?'

Chance gave him a wolf's smile. 'Yo!'

'Then do it!'

The big blond made it to the opposite wall and was just about to turn the corner, heading right, when a sudden fusillade from an off-white adobe building to the north ripped chunks out of the boards ahead of him. Chance almost fell back, cursing, then started firing back with his long gun.

'*Give him some cover!*' Frost yelled.

Boone and Forrest didn't need telling twice. As all three set up a wall of lead to keep the occupants of the long adobe building down, Chance turned and headed for the stable. A couple of heartbeats later he crashed into the high-roofed structure with enemy bullets chasing his heels.

Once inside he felt his guts loosen up a bit. In another second he was calm – deadly calm. A quick head-count revealed that there were sixteen horses in the livery, wall-eyed and spooked by all the gunfire. It was a simple enough matter to stampede them, and Chance was happy to oblige.

The horses burst out through the stable doors with Chance yelling and firing bullets into the rafters behind them. The chaos already in evidence in the courtyard abruptly became worse as the sudden river of horseflesh caused a stunned lull in the proceedings. For long moments the only sounds were the rumble of many hooves and the occasional wild gunshot.

Beneath the confusion, the Wilde boys began to move in for the kill.

Inside the long adobe building, Lieutenant Baxter regained consciousness with a start.

He lay trussed in the corner of the large, echo-filled room where the Black Wolf held court, wondering if the events of the past few days had all been a dream. The ambush at Firewater Creek and his capture by the very outlaws he had set out to track, his interrogation and torture … They were certainly the things from which nightmares

were made. But then he groaned. Pain and
discomfort confirmed the reality of his situation.
He winced.

And then, realising that he was not alone, his
head jerked up to find the Black Wolf looming
above him, the light of panic now filling his
bloodshot eyes. All at once the lieutenant realised
what had woken him.

The Black Wolf kicked him again.

'Thought you said you come here alone?' the
outlaw snarled. 'Happen that's true, who's those
sonsofbitches out there now, then, huh?'

Baxter lay still, lacking both the energy and the
inclination to move. He felt awful and looked
worse. His uniform was stained and torn, his eyes
swollen almost shut, his lips split and puffed and
his hair matted with blood from a dozen cuts.
Gradually his mind began to clear, but even the
thunder of gunfire outside, a sound upon which
his family had thrived for generations, failed to
stir him.

Gunfire?

That didn't make sense. But as he began to
frown, the Wolf reached down, grabbed him by the
tunic and hauled him to his feet. He held his face
so close to Baxter's that the young man could
smell pemmican and mescal on his breath.

'You better tell me jus' what it is you're playin'
at, boy,' he growled. 'An' you better tell me fast.'

The lieutenant shook his head, dazed.

'I don't think he knows, Josh.'

The Black Wolf dropped Baxter and spun to

face Bob Jarvis. He, like Will Slade, who stood by the door, was loaded for bear but badly shaken by the dawn raid.

'What you sayin'?' the Wolf demanded.

His consumptive partner shrugged. 'Just that I don't think the soldier-boy's got one clue 'bout who's out there.'

'Well who the hell *is* it, then? I don't buy coincidence. They *gotta* be connected to this sonofabitch.'

'Not ne...'

At that moment another explosion ripped through the brightening day and as the ground shook and plaster fell in a shower, the three outlaws flinched and turned towards the windows.

'What in hell ...?'

The sounds of battle outside grew louder.

Frost, Boone, Chance and Forrest used the cover of the stampeding horses to cross the courtyard and dive behind Baxter's payroll wagon, which had been parked twenty feet to the left of the fountain.

While Dark, McCord and Longblade continued to pour fire into the bunkhouse, O'Connor struck a match on his thumb-nail and took another stick of dynamite from his sack.

'Now what you gonna do?' asked Dark, wiping a smudge of dirt off his bloodless face.

The Irishman's green eyes twinkled. 'Flush 'em out,' he replied. Setting the match to the thin fuse protruding from the explosive, he added, 'Cover me!'

As soon as the three convicts began firing again, the NCO got to his feet and lobbed the sputtering stick towards the corner where the bunkhouse met the Black Wolf's quarters.

Four seconds ticked into history before the explosive blew, tearing a ragged chunk of masonry out of the adjoining walls. A tiny flame found something to feed on; smoke and dust mixed together to form a black, suffocating cloud. The whores started screaming louder and the outlaws, with no choice but to fight or die, came out shooting.

Soon the air was busy with lead. One black man firing a Spencer repeater for all it was worth hit O'Connor in the right bicep before Longblade sent him to Judgement with a barbed-tip arrow clogging his airway. The Irishman tumbled onto his back, rolled into a sitting position with his back to the fountain wall and hurriedly inspected the damage.

'You all right, sarge?'

'I'll live.'

Bullets zipped through the air. Forrest, fed up with trying to work his rifle with his ham-like fists, tossed the long gun away and ran after a group of four escaping outlaws with his bare hands held high.

'*Attaboy, partner!*' McCord yelled enthusiastically.

Forrest got six paces before he took a bullet in

the left leg. He buckled, stumbled, straightened up and kept on coming. His face was contorted by a yell of rage and his hair and beard flew madly around his face.

All but one of the outlaws scattered before he could reach them. The unlucky fellow was tall and heavy, but he didn't stand a chance against the former medicine-show strongman.

The other three owlhoots looked back just as Forrest picked up their *compadre*, held him aloft, then hurled him back into the burning bunkhouse via one of the shattered windows. Spooked, they continued their flight.

Or would have done, if Tom Boone hadn't been blocking their path.

The negro held his rifle barrel-down in his left hand. His teeth flared white in his ebony face. He sounded almost apologetic as he said, 'Best stand an' fight, fellers.'

That sounded fair. None of them were strangers to violence and bloodshed, after all. But as the outlaws began to lift their rifles, Boone's hand swooped to the butt of his .38 calibre Colt Lightning. The double-action handgun was up and blasting before the outlaws could properly recover themselves. They jerked under the impacting lead, then corkscrewed to the earth, dead or dying.

Frost covered the open ground between the wagon and the fountain in a zig-zagging run, firing his Winchester to keep enemy heads down. Reaching the fountain, he skidded to a halt and went down beside O'Connor.

There was no time for pleasantries. 'How bad is it?'

The NCO smiled. 'Looks worse than it is.'

'Good.' Frost glanced back over his shoulder just as Chance came out from behind the wagon, swinging his rifle like a club to scatter those outlaws still trying to find cover elsewhere, then returned his attention to the burning bunkhouse directly ahead. He said to McCord and Longblade, 'Get those whores out of there before the whole lot caves in. And keep an eye out for that lieutenant, if he's still alive.'

'Yo!'

As the two convicts circled the fountain, a big man with a scattergun came at McCord, yelling like a lunatic. The blue-eyed blond shot him in the stomach, but as the outlaw fell, his gun exploded. McCord yelled and joined him on the blood-stained ground. Longblade continued on and disappeared into the rapidly-growing inferno.

'How 'bout me, marshal?' asked Dark.

Frost blinked rapidly, then tore his eyes from McCord. There was no time for mourning right now. He indicated the Black Wolf's quarters with the still hot barrel of his rifle. 'We're going to take a look around in there.'

Dark spat. 'Aw shit. That's what I thought you was gonna say.'

Together, the two men straightened up and zig-zagged across the rubble-strewn courtyard, clattering to a halt in the shade of the porch overhang. Without waiting, Frost put the sole of his boot to the dusty door and it flew back on its hinges to slam against the inside wall. They entered a long, white-walled corridor hazy with disturbed dust. But no sooner had they set foot on the bare boards than a sudden blast of gunfire split the air. Both men went down into a crouch as splinters burst from the doorframe.

They caught one quick glimpse of Will Slade at the end of the corridor, then started shooting. Slade disappeared around a corner, leaving only a bullet-pocked wall behind him.

'Follow him,' Frost barked.

Dark looked grief-shot. '*You* follow 'im!'

Frost jacked another shell into his long gun. 'I got other fish to fry.' As he moved off in the opposite direction, heading down the corridor towards an arched doorway set in the opposite wall, Dark sighed.

With nothing better to do, he went after Slade.

He wasn't hard to find. Dark could still hear his high-heeled boots drumming against the boards as he tried to make a break for it. He followed cautiously, keeping his rifle aimed and ready, but when he peered around the corner, he saw only another empty corridor about fifteen feet long.

At the far end there was a plain white door that opened out into a narrow alley. Dark knew this because the door was only now swinging shut.

He approached it at a trot, cursing the clatter of his own boots on the floorboards. When he was close enough, he slowed and gingerly reached out with his rifle to push the door open again.

Almost at once a flurry of bullets tore splinters out of the panels. Dark jerked back, cursed, then threw himself out into the alleyway.

Will Slade stood about ten feet away with his legs apart and a Smith & Wesson .44 in his hand. For one split second his eyes met those of the albino. Then Dark shot him twice in the chest and Slade hit the dirt with his shoulder blades.

Frost slipped through the archway and into a long room with a high ceiling. Quickly he ran his eyes around it. Two tall windows, now shattered. A long table, now wearing a cloth of dust and rubble. Another door to his left. That was all.

No, not all.

The young soldier was trussed up like a slab of meat across the room in the far corner. Their eyes met briefly. Frost wasn't sure if the other man could even see him.

He was halfway across the room when a voice said, 'Hold it.'

He froze, then turned very slowly to face a man who looked more like a corpse.

'Bob Jarvis,' he said quietly.

The pale man in the dusty black suit stood in the doorway at the other end of the room, holding a Henry repeater in his bony hands. His skin was yellow and his breathing was ragged, no doubt aggravated by all the dust and smoke.

'Well, well, well,' he said in a quiet and dangerous tone. 'Hardly seems fair that you know me, but I don't know you, does it?' He moved a bit closer and asked with genuine curiosity, 'Who *are* you?'

Frost kept his eyes on the other man's trigger-finger. He forced his breathing to keep calm and steady. 'The man who's going to stop your clock,' he said softly.

He threw himself to one side just as Jarvis fired. Frost hit the floor, lost his grip on his rifle, rolled, heard the outlaw's second bullet strike the wall behind him and came up with his Colt New Line Police .38 in his hand.

He fired twice. The first shot hit Jarvis in the left breast, the second a little lower on the right. Crazy Bob staggered under the force of the bullets, opened his mouth to speak, spewed blood instead and fell face-down, already stiffening.

As the haze of gunsmoke cleared, Frost straightened to his full height and hurried across to the young lieutenant. Dimly he realised that the sounds of death and destruction outside were tapering off. One way or another, the battle was nearly over. He slipped his Colt back into leather and bent by the young man's side. Gently he rolled him over to untie the rope that held his arms halfway up his back.

'I … uh …'

'It's all right. Plenty of time for talk later.'

'But … who …?'

Frost loosened the rope and threw it over his shoulder, then eased Baxer's arms back to his sides and started rubbing them to revive the circulation.

And that was when the Black Wolf shot him.

One minute there was just the ragged, difficult breathing of the soldier as Frost worked on his wrists, the next the gunblast ripped apart the eerie silence settling over the monastery.

Frost loosed a cry of surprise and pain as the bullet gouged a burning slice out of his right shoulder and flew on to embed itself in the wall in front of him.

He turned and fell away just as the Wolf fired again. It was the first time the two adversaries had ever set eyes on each other. It would also be the last. Frost rolled again, clenching his teeth against the fire in his shoulder. The Black Wolf tracked him with the barrel of his Colt Wells Fargo. His black face was a twisted mask of fury, his eyes alive with insanity, and for the first time in his life – he was sweating.

He fired three .31 calibre bullets and each one tore into the floor where the grey-eyed marshal had been just seconds before. When he fired again and the gun clicked on empty, he hurled it at Frost but that missed, too.

With a snarl he drew the Bowie knife at his right hip. Frost scrabbled to his feet. His entire right arm was numb. He couldn't even feel the warmth of his blood pumping down it. Frantically he reached across with his left hand, trying to draw his Colt, but the Wolf cut the air before him and he had to pull back, forget about the gun and just concentrate on staying out of reach.

Again the Wolf made a gut-cutting sweep ahead

of him. Again Frost jerked back out of range, his eyes shuttling from the outlaw's knife-hand to his crazy, bloodshot eyes. He moved further back, two more steps, came up against a wall.

He was trapped.

Sensing victory, the Wolf gave a yell and drove in for the kill.

The boom of a long gun made both men flinch. It seemed to roar with cannon-like intensity. The Black Wolf staggered, came up straight, stared at Frost with a puzzled expression on his face and then spun around. Frost saw blood trickling from a hole in his back and puddling at his feet. Then he shifted his attention across to Lieutenant Baxter, now up on his knees with Frost's fallen Winchester in his unresponsive hands.

With another yell, this time more of pain than fury, the massive outlaw threw himself at the arched doorway, almost collapsing across his dead partner before he disappeared outside.

He burst into the body-littered courtyard and saw that everything had come to an end. The bunkhouse was a blazing inferno. The watch-tower had been blown into match-wood. The only bodies that he could see were those of his own men.

He came up sharp before the long adobe building from which he had plotted and planned his reign of terror and holding his knife high, gave a scream of defiance and rushed at those men still standing. His enemies.

They all saw him at the same time. Seven of them. And each man spun to shoot him at the same time, too.

Six bullets and one flint-headed arrow struck the black outlaw and tore him off his feet. He was already dead by the time he struck the adobe wall and slid down into a blood-spattered heap.

A few moments later, Frost and Baxter appeared in the doorway and glanced down at his body. The lieutenant seemed transfixed by the sight. Frost looked up as soon as he knew the Black Wolf wouldn't be stirring up any more trouble and stepped out into the new day.

O'Connor and the Wilde boys grinned at him. All of them.

'I thought we'd gotten rid of you,' Frost muttered to McCord.

The blue-eyed blond shrugged and looked down at his pellet-sprayed left arm. 'Sorry, marshal. Not this time.'

Frost turned his attention to the others. They were all smeared with blood and dust. Forrest was allowing a Mexican whore to bind his left leg. O'Connor had already received similar attention to his bullet-struck right arm. Only Boone, Chance and Longblade appeared unscathed.

'Where's Dark?' the marshal growled ominously.

As the Wilde boys turned to find out, the albino suddenly appeared from behind the parked wagon. He had a Mexican girl on his arm but for the moment seemed pre-occupied with something else.

'Hey, Frost. Is there somethin' you ain't told us

about this deal? There's a wagon here with a whole piss-pot full of money in it.'

A ripple went through the other men.

'News to me,' the marshal replied. 'But maybe the lieutenant here can shed some light on it.'

Baxter stepped forward. 'Indeed I can, sir.' Briefly, and swaying all the while, he told them how he came to be there. The men listened in disbelief.

'Well, lieutenant, you've retrieved your payroll,' Frost said at the end of it. 'And we'll make sure you get it back across the border in one piece.'

'Aw hell, Frost!'

'Shut it, Dark. You still owe us for saving your hide back in Spearman.'

'Yeah, but...'

'Longblade — go fetch the horses, will you? Chance — go help him. We'll have to round up a team for the wagon and a couple of spares for the, ah, *senoritas*, here.'

'Yo!'

As his men began to prepare for the journey home, Abel Frost heaved a sigh of relief. It was a despicable business they had been in, as con-men, thieves and killers. And yet it was their trade, and they acted accordingly. Death — how to inflict it and how to avoid it — was, above all else, the commodity in which they dealt. Whether by accident or design, it was the only way of life they knew.

But now Frost began to feel good about riding with them, for they were no longer animals in his eyes.

No. Now they were men.
Professionals.
Wilde boys.